Cover-Up in Columbus

by
Phil Hardwick

QUAIL RIDGE PRESS
Brandon, Mississippi

Printed in Canada

On the cover: Friendship Cemetery
Photo by Phil Hardwick

Illustrations by Phil Hardwick

Other books in Phil Hardwick's Mississippi Mysteries Series:

Found in Flora
Justice in Jackson
Captured in Canton
Newcomer in New Albany
Vengeance in Vicksburg
Collision in Columbia
Conspiracy in Corinth

To be included on the Mississippi Mysteries mailing list,
please send your name and complete mailing address to:

QUAIL RIDGE PRESS
P. O. Box 123 • Brandon, MS 39043
1-800-343-1583 • www.quailridge.com

ACKNOWLEDGMENTS

Many people took time to share their stories about Columbus and give me insight into the community. I also had the opportunity to become aware of several organizations working hard to ensure that downtown Columbus remains as the model for downtown revitalization in the United States. Not the least of these is the Main Street organization and its members. The news media, WCBI-TV and the *Commercial Dispatch* newspaper, have made a strong statement of their support of downtown by choosing to be in downtown.

Others served as experts in my research or otherwise provided valuable insight as I have gone about creating this story. I am grateful to them. They are:

Fred Bell	John Maxey
Sid and Brenda Caradine	Jan Miller
Bobby Delaughter	John Moffit, MD
Joe Fant	Ben Paulding
Birney Imes III	Will Sorey, MD
Pat and Sam Kaye	Nell Thomas
Susan Mackay	

As always, I acknowledge the wonderful support of the staff of Quail Ridge Press and that of my wife Carol.

● ● ●

If you would like more information about Columbus, call Main Street Columbus, Inc. at 662-328-6305, or the Columbus-Lowndes Chamber of Commerce at 662-328-4491.

Downtown Columbus

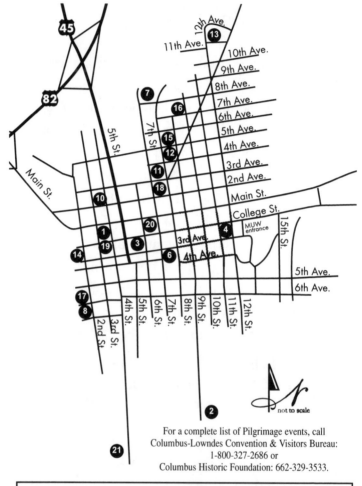

For a complete list of Pilgrimage events, call
Columbus-Lowndes Convention & Visitors Bureau:
1-800-327-2686 or
Columbus Historic Foundation: 662-329-3533.

TOUR 1	1	Welcome Center	**TOUR 4**	12	Harrison-Imes
	2	Rosedale		13	Magnolia Hill
	3	Arbor House		14	Twelve Gables
TOUR 2	4	Shadow Lawn	**TOUR 5**	15	Temple Heights
	5	Waverley (not shown)		16	Aldan Hall
	6	Amzi Love		17	Riverview
	7	Leighcrest		18	First Baptist Church
	8	Colonade		19	St. Paul's Episcopal Church
TOUR 3	9	Bryn Bella (not shown)		20	First United Methodist
	10	The Haven			Church
	11	Blewett-Harrison-Lee		21	Friendship Cemetery

PROLOGUE

The two gravediggers tossed their cigarettes beside their rubber boots and squished them in the wet ground when the first black Cadillac hearse rolled slowly through the arches of Friendship Cemetery. They studied the second vehicle that pulled in. It too was a Cadillac hearse. The men retreated with their shovels into the nearby woods, away from the graves they had dug.

It was the Tuesday after Thanksgiving. They had spent part of yesterday and all of this chilly November morning preparing the two plots. When the mist began floating down earlier, the older of the two men had cursed. Funerals in the rain can be trouble for gravediggers when the ground gets too moist. He should know. He had dug over four hundred graves in this cemetery. It was his assistant's first week on the job. The funeral procession crept closer.

"Don't think I ever seen a funeral with two hearses," said the young gravedigger.

"There's lots of 'em," said the older man. "Usually car accidents."

"Was this a car wreck?"

"Nope. This is Mr. Newberry and his youngest son. They both died on Thanksgiving Day. Now it's time for us to hush up and get behind this big oak tree."

The two hearses parked in the proper spot just past

the large, dark green funeral home tent, and with military precision the drivers got out and opened the back doors of each hearse. They stood solemnly as the remainder of the procession snuggled tightly to a stop along the narrow asphalt streets of the old cemetery. Squeaky windshield wipers went silent one pair at a time. Doors opened and closed. Pallbearers made their way, removed the caskets from the compartments of the hearses, and placed them on chrome-plated devices that would lower the steel boxes into the vaults of the final resting places.

The crowd gathered around the Newberry family plot, and the minister performed the graveside service. Ashes to ashes, dust to dust. Some thought the service went a little faster than dignity allowed. Others were grateful for a brief graveside service because the mist was turning into rain droplets, and it was time to get back to work. For others, a lunch of turkey sandwiches and cornbread dressing awaited at home.

Chapter 1

"I just want to make sure that his death was an accident. That's all."

It was a windy March Monday morning in Mississippi, a few minutes after ten. Erica Newberry

Castle was leaning forward in a high-backed chair in the sitting room of the elegant Edison Walthall Hotel in downtown Jackson, making her case to private detective Jack Boulder.

She had gotten up early this morning and driven two and half hours on Interstate 20 from Tuscaloosa. Along the way she was comforted when she noticed the dogwood blooms in the woods alongside the busy four-lane, divided highway. Not a particularly religious woman, she knew the story of the dogwood from her Sunday school days as a young girl growing up in Columbus, Mississippi. The cross on which Jesus was crucified was said to have been made from a dogwood tree. After His death and resurrection, future dogwood trees grew short and gnarled, and the white bloom was stained blood red so that the world would remember His death. The blooms occurred in the springtime of course, just in time for Easter Sunday. She didn't really believe the story, but as she drove along among the eighteen-wheel trucks and saw the blooming trees, it somehow gave her comfort that she was doing the right thing by having the death of her youngest brother investigated. Every day since Thanksgiving she had thought about her younger brother and the way he had died. She needed closure to the case, but feared that finding the truth might make her life more miserable. What if her older brother had killed her younger brother?

She had let the matter go on too long without doing

anything. A fellow college faculty member had finally come to her in her crowded little office and said, "Whatever is bothering you is changing you from the person you used to be." That was when she made the decision to hire a private investigator. She figured hiring a local Columbus detective would not be a good idea because everybody knows everything about everybody in a small town. Besides, everybody in Columbus had long ago formed an opinion about the case. An Alabama investigator would be good, but an out-of-state detective might not have the necessary contacts. So she called the directory assistance operator for area code 601 and asked for the telephone number of the first private detective in the Yellow Pages in Jackson, Mississippi. She was given the name and number of Andrew Jackson Boulder.

The private investigator sat across from her and leaned back in his comfortable sitting chair. He knew nothing about her situation and assumed that the woman in front of him had been referred by one of his big insurance company clients. Boulder's cases usually came from such sources. His ego would have been dented slightly if he knew that this prospective client had selected him by random chance. He prided himself on being able to take only cases that appealed to him. Fortunately he did not need to exist on divorce cases or custody disputes. He despised domestic matters. He had seen enough of those in his years as a St. Louis homicide detective. His retirement to Jackson, Mississippi, was working out nicely. He was maintaining his 188 pounds, his same weight when he graduated from the police academy over twenty years ago. He took only one case at a time. The third bedroom of his downtown condominium was his office, and the quality of his clients was on the upswing. His personal life was also changing. He was actually beginning to enjoy some things he used to think were highbrow, things such as going to plays and symphony concerts. Just last week he and his girlfriend Laura had gone to New Stage Theater to see "Forever Plaid." Watch out Mississippi Symphony Orchestra!

Ah, Laura—his high school sweetheart with whom he had become reacquainted upon moving back to Jackson. Early in his adult life he'd had a brief marriage with no children, and she'd had the same experience. She was now a high-powered attorney with a law firm that occupied two floors of the tallest building in town. They were best friends and more. But a problem was developing. Boulder was letting the unthinkable happen. He was falling in love with Laura. What he needed was a good case to occupy his mind and get him out of town awhile. Maybe this one would fit the bill. He had the time.

Boulder studied the woman. She wore black slacks, a peach-colored turtleneck, and a black fleece vest. Her hair was medium length and styled in the wet look that was popular nowadays. She was thirty-nine, but had the skin of a twenty-nine year old, which made her excessive makeup look even heavier than it was. She was fit and trim, but not tan. That meant she probably worked out at a health club, although with it being early spring, she could be a jogger and still have pale skin. Her nails were painted in a glossy dark cherry color, and her lipstick was a blood red that looked maroon. Boulder used to be able to guess what a woman did by the way she dressed. He gave up such presumptions a long time ago. At least he liked to think he did. He was already mentally guessing her occupation.

"What would make you think otherwise?" asked Boulder.

"My younger brother Benji was killed in a hunting accident this past Thanksgiving," she began. "It happened in Lowndes County on some property that our family owns. They say that he was killed by our eleven-year-old nephew, but I find it hard to believe that even a child would shoot at someone who was wearing those orange vests they wear when they go hunting. I just want to find out what really happened is all."

"Do you have any reason to believe it wasn't an accident?"

"There have been a lot of rumors. Our father was a relatively wealthy man. There are two other brothers and they have never liked Benji. They have always been jealous of him, and our father seemed to like Benji more the last few years."

"What did Benji do for a living?" asked Boulder.

"He was a photographer. Actually one might say that he was a small business owner. He had a studio on Main Street in Columbus. He exhibited his work on the street floor. You could buy calendars with his photos, posters, and framed pictures. He also sold a lot of his work on the Internet. He lived in an apartment upstairs. He had two employees who helped him run the studio, but his true love was photography. He was out shooting most of the time. He shot everything—sports, nature scenes, sunsets, boats on the Tennessee-Tombigbee, you name it. He even received awards for his work. The studio provided a way for him to do what he really wanted to do."

"What about his social life?"

"Benji wasn't really a shy person, but he was reserved. If he had a choice, he would rather be alone than with a group of people."

"Ever been married?"

"Me?"

"No," said Boulder. "Benji."

"No."

"Was he a hunter?"

"No," she said, her voice becoming firm. "He went hunting once a year. Norman, our older brother, has always had a deer hunt on Thanksgiving morning. I stand corrected. Our father started the tradition. Every Thanksgiving morning, the men would go out on the deer stands and hunt while the women would prepare dinner. Then during the meal they would talk about deer hunting and then go watch some silly football game like most men do. Benji hated Thanksgiving at our house just as much as I did. He once told me that he went to the deer stand and just sat there. He could never kill an animal."

"What do you do for a living, Ms. Castle?"

"I am an English professor at the University of Alabama," she replied.

"When did you leave Columbus?"

"In the eleventh grade," she said. Boulder thought he detected a touch of melancholy in her voice. "My parents sent me to a girls' boarding school in Massachusetts, then I attended Radcliffe, where I majored in English Literature. I took a Master's from Yale and then went to work."

"At the university?"

"Are you kidding?" she said with a laugh. "I was a flight attendant based in New York for three years. I finally decided I wanted to come back to the South where life was a bit more real."

"I know what you mean."

She reached in her small, black purse and pulled out a piece of paper and a business card that identified her as Erica N. Castle, Ph.D., English Department, University of Alabama. "Here are the names and addresses of my family members in Columbus. I told them I was going to hire a private detective and that they would be contacted. They laughed, of course."

"So you think one of them killed Benji?"

"Let's just say I don't think my nephew killed him," she said.

"So tell me a little more about your family," said Boulder.

"Ah, my family," she said. "Could we go to the restaurant and get a cup of coffee? This might take a few minutes."

"Of course."

They got up and went down the hall to the hotel restaurant. They were alone except for the kitchen staff setting up a lunch buffet that would soon bring in a full house of diners. Their server brought two black coffees, and they sipped as she told the abbreviated family story.

"I'm a member of the Newberry family of Columbus. Granddaddy started it all back in the thirties when he opened a sawmill just outside of town. He bought lots of land with lots of trees and eventually added a lumber supply store. My father came back from World War II and built Newberry Lumber into a chain of lumber supply houses all over the South."

"I've heard of them," noted Boulder, thinking that this was bigger money than he had realized.

"Daddy was all business and was extremely disappointed when not even one of his children had the least desire to run the family business. We kids got Mother's personality genes. She was artistic, eccentric, and carefree, but a little snobbish at the same time. Daddy was just the opposite. We grew up in a large house. No, it was a mansion. Daddy's office was in the lumber company, and he dealt with sweaty men who cursed and drank a lot when they were not working. Daddy bailed more than one of them out of jail on the weekends. None of us was turned on to that."

"Tell me about your brothers."

"The oldest brother is Norman. He would be about fifty-four now. Norman is a real estate broker, but mostly he manages the family land. He has a wife named Earlene, who thought she was going to be living in a mansion like a Newberry when she married the oldest son. They live in a glorified cabin in the woods so he can hunt and fish when he wants to. A year after they married, they found out she couldn't have any children."

"Next is Nathanial, or Nate, as everybody calls him. He's married to Annie, who owns a beauty shop downtown, and they have one son, Robbie. He's the one who was on the hunt that day and supposedly shot Benji."

"What kind of work does Nate do?" asked Boulder.

"He manages Newberry Furniture Store. It's more upscale than a lumber store, if you know what I mean."

The server poured more coffee and asked if they were having lunch. They declined and Boulder noticed that the early lunch crowd was beginning to file in.

"Then there is Benji, bless his heart," she continued.

"He's thirty-six, I mean was thirty-six, which is three years younger than I. When he was growing up, Benji had older brothers that were almost twenty years older, so he didn't relate much to them. He and I were best friends as kids. He told me everything. Anyway, Benji got a degree from Ole Miss, then sort of job-hopped during his twenties. He finally settled down and, as I said, opened a photo shop on Main Street. Photography was his passion."

"Tell me again why this might not be an accident."

"Daddy had some heart problems last year and had bypass surgery. Ever since his heart attack he thought every day would be his last. He changed his will so that Benji would get most of his estate."

"Why would he do that?" asked Boulder.

"When Daddy was in the hospital, Benji went and sat with him every day. Norman and Nate seldom stopped by. Daddy took it personally, I'm afraid."

"How did you find out about him changing his will?"

"Mother called. She felt like she needed to tell the children," said Erica Newberry Castle.

"How did that make Norman and Nate and Erica feel?"

"Norman and Nate were very upset. They called me and asked if I would go with them to Daddy and confront him about changing his will. I declined, but they went ahead anyway. Daddy would only tell them that they would find out when he dies. He told them to get out and then went into the bedroom where Mother was and threw a lamp on the floor. Mother said he cursed like one of his lumberjacks and that she was afraid he was going to have another heart attack right then and there."

"So," said Boulder, adding a long pause. "We have a death and a motive, and if it's not accidental, we have some suspects."

She nodded slowly.

"If it's not accidental, do you really want to know who killed Benji?"

"No," she said, as her eyes reddened with tears. "I just want to know if it's an accident, that's all."

He handed her a table napkin and said, "Then I'm sorry. You've come to the wrong man. Mississippi families may keep their secrets buried in their own little gardens, but I was a homicide detective for over twenty years in St. Louis, Missouri. I'm interested in justice, not uncovering family secrets, Mrs. Castle." He stood up, reached in his pocket, and laid a five dollar bill on the table. "You'll need to find someone else."

"Wait, please," she pleaded. "I'm sorry. Sit back down. I didn't mean what I said."

Boulder looked down at her and saw a tired, confused woman who was on the verge of coming apart.

"What did you mean?"

"I just don't know if I can handle it if brother killed brother. But you're right. There must be justice and I must know. I'm sorry." She reached into her purse and handed him an envelope. "Please go ahead with your investigation. Here is a retainer fee and expense money. Please charge me your usual fee when that runs out."

Boulder glanced down into a fat envelope and saw nothing but hundred dollar bills. "How much is in here?"

"Five thousand. My address and telephone number are in there as well. Is that enough?"

"I think it will get me started. There is just one more thing."

"You said your last name was Castle. I don't see a wedding band. What happened to your husband?"

"He was killed in a hunting accident several years ago."

Chapter 2

On Wednesday, Jack Boulder had lunch with his girl-friend Laura and briefed her on his meeting with Erica Newberry Castle. Usually she listened patiently when he told her about his cases, just as he listened patiently to her when she told him about her cases. She seemed to be especially interested in this case. There was the potential for complex legal issues, she told him. A lawyer likes that.

In the middle of the afternoon, he packed a bag with several days of casual clothing and struck out for Columbus in his fully restored 1968 Chevrolet Camaro, a tangible manifestation of his nostalgia for a time in his life when he first experienced real freedom. In America, the automobile represents freedom. For Boulder, that came when he got his first car. His Camaro was not particularly noteworthy as far as the model went. It had a 327 cubic-inch engine, a four-speed transmission, an AM radio, and a heater. Its distinctive feature was a rally stripe around its nose. Boulder had noticed the retro trend in today's car market. He was also aware that his car got noticed most places he went. For a private detective, that can be a disadvantage, so he only drove it on cases such as this one where everybody knew who he was and why he was there. For his other cases, an arrangement with a local rental car company worked just fine.

Two and a half hours later he crossed the Tennessee-Tombigbee Waterway on U.S. 82, just south of the spot where Hernando DeSoto and his band of a thousand men presumably crossed in 1541 enroute from Florida to the Mississippi River. The "Tenn-Tom," one of the largest public works projects in American history, was completed in 1984 after twelve years of construction and a cost of nearly two billion dollars. Through massive land-moving, trenching, and lock and dam construction, the Tombigbee River was joined with the Tennessee River to create a water route that took 800 miles off the trip from mid-America to the Gulf of Mexico.

Unlike many Mississippi cities, the homes of Columbus were not destroyed in the Civil War. The town served as a hospital center, an arsenal, a major food-producing center, and even as state capital for a brief moment in time. The stately, columned mansions of Columbus became an attraction in the 1940s when city leaders created an official pilgrimage during April of each year. The South Columbus Historic District is a cohesive, well-preserved neighborhood of architecturally and historically significant buildings that visually illustrate the city's historical pattern of development.

If a feature story researcher stood on the corner of Main Street and Fifth Street under "the clock" and asked a hundred passersby what Columbus was known for, there would be at least a dozen different categories of responses. Some would say that the city is best-known for being the birthplace of the Pulitzer Prize-winning playwright Tennessee Williams. Others would point out that Columbus is the site of the country's first Memorial Day on April 25, 1866. The fact that Columbus is home of Franklin Academy, the first public school in Mississippi, would be referred to. Still others would proclaim Columbus as the home of Mississippi University for Women, founded in 1884, the first state-supported institution of higher learning for women in the country. Also noted would be Columbus

Air Force Base, where pilots in training come to fly the T-38 Talon. The researcher's list would be long and include festivals, celebrations, and historic homes. And, of course, the Pilgrimage, which Boulder would discover was about to begin in only a few days.

He took the exit labeled "downtown" and followed the signs to the Welcome Center, a soft blue and butterscotch two-story Victorian home built in 1878 and the birthplace of Tennessee Williams. He went inside and was greeted by an attractive receptionist.

"Do you have a listing of bed and breakfast facilities in town?" he inquired.

"We sure do," she said, handing him a colorful brochure.

Boulder studied a list that included Amzi Love, Arbor House, Highland House, and Liberty Hall. He raised his head and asked, "Any recommendations?"

"Oh, sir, they are all very fine accommodations."

A diplomatic reply, but it didn't help Boulder. He decided to do something he did not usually do—select the first one on the list. "How about the Amzi Love House?"

"I'm sure you will find it most satisfactory," she said. "Are you in town for the Market Street Festival?"

"No," he said softly.

"The Pilgrimage?"

"No. I'm here on business, but I'm not sure how long I'll be here," said Boulder.

"Well, you need to stay for those two things," she said enthusiastically. "You'll be glad you did."

"Did Tennessee Williams really live in this house?" asked Boulder.

"Oh certainly. Only it's been moved a block to this spot. It was the rectory at St. Paul's Episcopal Church. His grandfather was the rector there."

"Here's a package of information about Columbus and all the things to do while you're here. And I hope your business here is successful."

"Thank you," said Boulder. "So do I."

He drove to the Amzi Love House, located at 305 Seventh Street South, and was greeted by a perky woman in her late twenties who introduced herself as Katherine and told him to "make yourself at home" in the living room while she took care of "some business in the kitchen." She wore a gray jogging suit that had

"M.U.W." printed on the front of the jersey. He sat down on the sofa, picked up a booklet published by the Columbus-Lowndes County Convention and Visitors Bureau entitled "Where Flowers Healed A Nation" and read an article about the house:

The history of the Amzi Love House has remained intact, for this home has been occupied by descendants of the builder for about 150 years now. By America's vagabond standards, such stability is most unusual. The house is now the residence of the eighth generation of Amzi's descendants. They run it as a bed and breakfast inn and have welcomed more than a few internationally known writers and media people.

Lawyer Amzi Love built the house for his bride, Edith Wallace. The 1848 Greek Revival/Gothic Revival "cottage" is not a cottage at all; rather it is a house built to a smaller scale. And so are the furnishings, many of which are original to the house. The house has changed very little over the years. For example, the back porch was once enclosed with stationary louvered doors; it is now enclosed with glass. The sidelights feature beautiful Venetian glass, original to the house. The lawn offers a pretty and shady spot for garden parties, receptions, or jazz brunches, a favorite of the owners.

The Amzi Love is a Pilgrimage home, a popular B&B, a place for weddings and receptions, and is open for tours on selected days.

She returned shortly and Boulder paid for Wednesday and Thursday nights in advance. Friday and Saturday were already booked. He inquired about places to eat dinner.

"I'll give you three choices and you can decide," said Katherine. "There's Harvey's, which is a great place for steaks, et cetera; Ruben's, which is a catfish restaurant down by the river, and then there is Katherine's famous pimento cheese sandwiches, chips and a glass of wine. The good news on the last one is that you don't have to leave the house. The price is right too, but you might get what you pay for."

"Sounds like door number three can't be beat," said Boulder.

She showed him to his room and he unpacked while she prepared the sandwiches. Boulder noticed that there were at least two other couples staying in the house. He

went back to the kitchen and sat down at the counter while Katherine prepared the food.

"Do you own the house?" asked Boulder.

"No. I'm just helping out the owners until Friday. I come in and sort of take over when they are out of town. In real life, I'm a website designer. I work out of my apartment and have clients all over the world."

"Sounds like the hours are flexible," he remarked.

"That's what's so great about it. And I just love where I live."

"And where is that?"

"In a second floor studio apartment on Main Street with a ceiling that is twelve feet high and a Siamese cat named Snickers who loves to sit in the window and watch the cars go by below. I was lucky to get the apartment last year. They have a waiting list, you know."

"I didn't know that," said Boulder.

"Oh yes," she said. "They have had this incredible downtown revitalization thing in Columbus, and there are now about sixty or seventy renovated second floor apartments downtown."

"Do you happen to know Benji Newberry?"

"I know who he is. I've seen him at one of our association meetings. He's from old Columbus money. He got killed, you know."

She pulled two plates from the cabinet and loaded them with sandwiches and chips and led him into the dining room. They sat down, tipped their glasses to each other, and began munching on their sandwiches. He told her that he had been hired to investigate Benji's death. Boulder figured she would close up at the mention of that fact, but, to the contrary, she became even more talkative.

"The Newberrys aren't the richest family in Columbus, but they hold their own with the aristocrats, if you know what I mean. The mother is the one that gets me. If I didn't know better, I would swear that she has a neck deformity that causes her to keep her nose stuck up in the air all the time. She would not be caught dead at a table that had a pimento cheese sandwich on it."

Boulder laughed and said, "One of those dinner party people, huh?"

"Oh, you don't know the half of it," said Katherine. "I will give credit where credit is due, however. If there is one thing Mrs. Ethel Newberry does well, it is throw a brunch. They have this group that calls itself the World Club, also referred to as the refined ladies of society in Columbus. There can only be twelve of them in the club. The youngest is sixty-six. Every week for over thirty years now, the refined ladies of Columbus have met at each others' homes for brunch and conversation. Although some might prefer to call it gossip, they have turned talk of others into an art form. They never mention anyone by name, instead referring to a person's occupation or attributes. For example, Rev. Colton is 'a certain gentleman who rises to the pulpit on Sunday mornings,' and Mary Morgan the insurance agent is 'that lady who drives the gray Volvo and feels it necessary to work at a trade.' The primary requirements for membership in the refined ladies of Columbus are at least one trip outside of North America, a pedigree of at least two generations—it used to be three—and not working outside the home.

"One week back in the fifties when it was Ethel Newberry's turn to host the meeting, she announced that she would be presenting a new shrimp salad dish that contained just a touch of curry. She was certain it would be the envy of the group and be talked about for weeks. There would also be shrimp cocktail, butterflied grilled shrimp, shrimp remoulade, and shrimp dip. In accordance with the rules of the club, there was no fried shrimp because fried foods were banned from most of the diets of the refined ladies. She personally prepared the shrimp salad and told everyone that it had been served on the finest silver platters in New Orleans and that it would be her honor to introduce it to the World Club of Columbus.

"On the appointed day when the ladies were about to arrive at the Newberry mansion, she made one final check and to her horror discovered that her cat had somehow gotten on the table and was feasting on the shrimp salad. She yanked up the cat with both hands and threw it and its shrimp salad tainted whiskers on the back porch. She returned to the dining room and saw the first guest walking up the sidewalk to her front door. In a panic, she grabbed a spoon and scooped out the part around where the cat had eaten. As the doorbell was ringing, she smoothed out the shrimp salad, then welcomed her guest as if nothing had happened. Soon, the rest of the ladies arrived and had a sumptuous brunch, all the while raving on the shrimp salad and begging for the recipe. Mrs. Newberry smiled through it all and told them that she was sworn to secrecy by the New Orleans chef who gave it to her, but on her next trip to the Crescent City would make every effort to get permission to reveal the recipe even if she had to bat her eyes for the Cajun gastronome. The ladies loved it and went away with all the attention being left on Mrs. Newberry and the shrimp salad.

"She bid farewell to the last guest and then went to the back porch, where she found her cat dead as could be laying on its side. In a fright she did the only thing she could do, and immediately called the ladies one by one confessing that the cat had gotten in the shrimp salad and that she had covered up the sin only to find the cat was now deceased and insisting that they all go immediately to the hospital and have their stomachs pumped to remove the tainted shrimp salad. At the hospital they still talk about the day that the dozen refined ladies of Columbus were spilling their insides in the emergency room.

"Well, after the ordeal Mrs. Newberry returned home

and went to the back porch to put the cat in a box. Her neighbor walked up and in a sympathetic voice told Mrs. Newberry that the cat had been run over by the car while her husband was backing out the driveway and that they didn't know what to do, so they just laid the cat on the back porch."

"That was a good story," said Boulder. He was still grinning.

"It says more about Ethel Newberry than anything else I could tell you."

"I usually jog every morning," he said. "Do you have a route you could recommend?"

"You are in good jogging territory if you like old houses and historic schools. I recommend you head out the front door, do a U-turn to the right, and head down to M.U.W., then come back up Third Avenue. Stay on it until it runs into Riverfront." She was using her right arm and hand as a directional compass while she spoke. "You'll see lots of great house styles in the Southside neighborhood, and you will really like it down on Riverfront. The big mansion with the white columns is the Newberry mansion. You can't miss it."

Boulder pointed to her jersey and said, "Is that your school?"

"You bet," she said with pride. "The campus is very historic. In fact, I think there are twenty-four buildings on the National Registry of Historic Places. When the W opened back in the eighteen-eighties, it was the first public college for women in the nation. Lately, we get attention because we're ranked number one as a best value among southern liberal arts colleges."

"What was your major?"

"Art," she said. "With a minor in business."

"And now you're a website designer?"

"A good combination of both degrees, I think."

"I agree," he said. "Thanks for the meal and the conversation. I'd better be getting to my room."

They got up and she said, "On your jog, be sure to run under the Old Maid's Gate. I think it's supposed to bring you luck or something. They call it The Portal now. The rumor is that if a new female student walks through it forward instead of backward, she will be an old maid. However, if a girl accidentally walks though

it forward, she can kiss the big rock that is just past it, and the spell will be taken away."

"I'll be sure to run through it."

Chapter 3

The next morning Boulder had breakfast at the Amzi Love House, making sure to tell Katherine that last evening's meal was one of the most enjoyable he had experienced lately. He jogged the route suggested by Katherine and was not disappointed. If Oscar Wilde wanted a setting for *Our Town,* this was it. Afterwards he showered and dressed and headed downtown.

He drove to the local office of the Department of Wildlife, Fisheries and Parks, where he found Warden Clifford Remington in the break room with his elbows on a table and sipping from a styrofoam cup of black coffee.

"Hello, Warden. I'm Jack Boulder." The visitor extended his right hand and laid a white business card on the table with his left hand. Remington kept the cup to his lips, letting the coffee vapors rise around the top half of his face. He stared at Boulder as if he were watching a television screen. "I've been hired to investigate the death of Benji Newberry." He let the words hang.

"Sit down," said Remington, still not moving the white cup.

"I understand you were the first one on the scene the morning he was shot."

"That would be correct."

"Can you tell me about it?" asked Boulder.

"Got an hour and a half?"

"Well, sure," said Boulder, pulling out the heavy red plastic chair in front of him and sitting down.

Remington stood straight up, leaving the coffee cup sitting on the table and revealing a frame of over six feet. Boulder guessed he did not weigh over one hundred sixty pounds. His most prominent feature was his Adam's apple, which from Boulder's lower position looked like an arrowhead stuck in the warden's throat.

"Let's go," said Remington. "I'll drive."

Boulder followed Remington out the back door to a green Jeep Cherokee with the agency's emblem displayed on the doors. They got in and Remington drove through city streets and finally headed south on the main highway. After twenty minutes of driving on progressively smaller and narrower roads, they turned onto a dirt road that led into a forest heavily thickening with the leaves of the new season. After a half-mile they came to a pipeline right-of-way that cut a fifty-foot wide clearing through the woods.

"They all came in one car, which they parked right over there in the woods," said Remington, pointing off to the right. "When I got the call, I drove to this spot right where we sit. I looked down the pipeline and saw a man waving both arms at me, flapping like a chicken. I drove straight to him."

Remington put the Jeep in gear and started driving slowly down the right-of-way. He stopped at a certain point, turned off the ignition, and stepped outside.

"I recognized him right away as Norman Newberry. He said that his brother had been accidentally shot."

"Did he use that word—accidentally?" asked Boulder.

"Not exactly. He said 'There's been an accident. My brother's been shot.' They were gathered around that tree and the younger brother was spread out on the ground."

"Was he face up, face down, or on his side?" asked Boulder.

"Face up," replied Remington. "He was spread out, feet real far apart. He had on an orange hunting vest and there was a hole right through the middle of it. He had already turned blue."

"Were they giving him CPR?"

"No. They said they tried, but gave up when he did-n't come around."

"Show me where they said they were when the shooting started."

Boulder followed as Remington backed up to the middle of the right-of-way. The warden placed his hands on his hips and looked to his right, then his left. Boulder sensed that he was re-creating Thanksgiving morning.

"From where we are now standing, I would say that Nate was about fifty yards up the line on the western side of the line and that Norman was about thirty yards down the line on the eastern side, which was the same side as the boy."

"What about the boy?"

"That's what makes no sense. He was right in front of Benji across the line."

Boulder walked over to the spot where the boy would have been, turned around and looked across the line, studying the thick woods in front of him, imagining what they would have looked like on the morning of the accident. The warden ambled over and stood beside him.

"Now according to the brothers," said the warden, "a good-sized buck came walking down the edge of the line on the side the boy was on. Nate took the first shot and hit the deer in the rump, which caused the animal to take off running. He ran diagonally down the line right toward where Benji was sitting. When he got right in front of Benji, the boy shot and missed the deer, which kept running and then was shot at by Norman, who missed it. Then they looked and saw Benji on the ground."

"What was Benji wearing, other than a hunting vest?" asked Boulder.

"Good question. Unlike his older brothers, who were wearing camouflage suits, he wore blue jeans, hiking boots, and a jacket."

"What about his gun?"

"I'll be honest with you," said the warden, taking off his cap and sliding his fingers through oily brown hair. "I don't think I saw that he had a gun. But he did have two cameras. They were strapped around his neck and shoulders bandoleer-style."

"So what happened next?"

"The ambulance got here about ten minutes after I did. They loaded him up and off it went. I called the coroner and told him what I had, then he went to the hospital. I think the main concern of everybody was protecting the boy. They were worried how the boy would take it."

"Has anyone contacted you since then?"

"No. I guess not. I filed my report with my boss and that was that. Looked like another stupid hunting accident. I mean, who would put a boy that young thirty yards in front of someone else? That part doesn't make sense."

"Do you know the Newberrys?"

"Do I know the Newberrys? Man, everybody knows the Newberry brothers. I guess I knew Norman better than the others. Being a big outdoorsman, he was always showing me his deer or fish. He pulled many bass over ten pounds out of the river. He held the record for the biggest deer in the state for awhile."

"Sounds like he was a good hunter."

"Are you kidding? He could tell where a deer was going to eat before the deer knew."

"Was he a good marksman?" asked Boulder.

"Norman Newberry could pop a gnat off the ear of a bobcat at fifty yards and never make it flinch."

They got back in the Jeep and rode back to Columbus in silence.

Chapter 4

The waiting room of Joseph Nettles, M.D. was functional. There were thirty padded chrome chairs, several rounded coffee tables, and ample copies of outdoor, women's, and weekly news magazines. In short, it was like hundreds of other physicians' waiting rooms.

Jack Boulder sat quietly, thumbing through a Mississippi fishing magazine that featured an article about angling for the big ones on the Tenn-Tom Waterway. According to the story, the best places to catch big channel catfish were the old riverbeds in the curves left when the Tombigbee River was straightened into its present configuration. He couldn't understand why anyone in his right mind would desire to go "grappling," a fishing technique that involved sticking one's arm into logs and other hiding places. The idea was to feel the fish and then grab it by the mouth and pull it out. This was done mostly at night. Nevertheless, a slew of fishermen in the article sang its praises. Boulder thought that a better use of the Tenn-Tom would be a houseboat cruise from Columbus to Mobile with Laura.

"Jack Boulder," came the announcement over the speaker in the ceiling. "Mr. Jack Boulder." He felt like he was in an airport about to take off somewhere. He got up and walked over to the glass window with the hole in it and was informed that Dr. Nettles would see him now. The receptionist did not seem irritated that he had shown up without an appointment, nor did it bother her when he told her that his visit was not for an examination. Perhaps Dr. Nettles had frequent visits from pharmaceutical salespeople. Boulder doubted that the receptionist took him for a salesperson in his outfit of dark chinos and white polo shirt. Maybe she thought he was a golfing buddy.

Boulder was ushered down the hall and into Dr. Nettles' office, a contemporary-looking space that was painted white and decorated light. The private investigator had expected dark paneling and a pedestal globe in the corner. The doorknob clicked and Boulder turned around to see a dark-haired man in his early thirties wearing casual pants and a white smock with his name stitched in blue.

"I'm Dr. Nettles," he announced, remaining in the

doorway. "What can I do for you?"

Boulder handed him a business card and said, "I'm investigating the death of Benji Newberry. I understand that you were on duty at the emergency room on Thanksgiving morning when he was brought in."

"Yes, that's right," said the physician, moving to his desk.

"Could I ask you a few questions? It won't take a minute."

The doctor looked down at his wristwatch, sat down in his chair and said, "Sure. If it will only take a few minutes."

"Please describe the condition of Mr. Newberry when he was brought to the hospital."

There was an urgent knock on the door, and a nurse stuck her head in the room and said, "Sorry to bother you, doctor, but we need you in Room Three, stat."

"Excuse me," said the doctor. He got up quickly and left the room.

Boulder studied the plaques on the wall and the photographs on the credenza behind the desk. Judging by these items, Joseph Yelverton Nettles, M.D. attended the University of Texas, Vanderbilt Medical School, and the United States Navy, in that order. Perhaps the Navy paid for medical school. There was a photo of an attractive blonde and two girls who looked elementary school age. Twenty minutes later, Dr. Nettles returned.

"Sorry about that. A child hyperventilated after

receiving an injection, and we wanted to make certain that it wasn't a reaction. Anyway, you were asking about Mr. Newberry?"

"Yes, go ahead."

"He arrived by ambulance shortly before noon. I would need to check the records for the exact time. He was deceased. Apparent cause of death was cardiac arrest based on the statements of his family members."

"Heart attack?" said Boulder quickly. "I thought he died from a gunshot wound."

"Oh, my mistake. You meant Benji. He arrived shortly before his father. He was also dead on arrival. Apparent cause of death was a gunshot wound to the chest. I was informed that it was a hunting accident. I immediately called the coroner, as is always the case when a gunshot wound is present. He came to the hospital and talked to the others, then did his examination. His conclusion was that death was caused by an accidental gunshot wound to the chest."

"Did he do an autopsy?"

"No."

"Isn't that unusual?" asked Boulder.

"I would say no in a case like this."

"What was the gunshot wound like? Rifle or shotgun?"

"An entry wound consistent with a four-ten gauge slug," said Dr. Nettles.

"Did you remove the slug?"

"No. Normally I would, even if there was no autopsy, but this was an unusual case."

"How so?"

"Nate and Norman told me privately that Nate's son had accidentally shot Benji. They were afraid that if the son knew that he had accidentally killed someone, it would seriously upset him. Maybe even psychologically scar the boy for life. They said that lots of shots were fired, and they wanted the boy to think that Norman had fired the shot by accident. Apparently, they convinced the boy of that. The kid kept telling Norman that everything would be alright. Norman did a good acting job."

"Do you know the Newberry family very well?"

"I know Nate well. He lives next door to me, and our kids play together. Norman is someone I know, but not as well."

"How about Mr. Newberry, the father?"

"I know only what I've heard. He was a very successful businessman, influential in state politics, and from one of the old Columbus families. I understand that he had a heart attack about a year ago, but I was not his physician. Apparently he had not been in good health since then."

"So who died first—the father or the son?"

"I couldn't tell you," said the physician. "All I can say is that Benji came in first, and then his father came in shortly thereafter."

"Do you consider that unusual?"

"Statistically, the odds of a father and son dying on the same day in separate locations would be about the same as winning the lottery in Florida."

Chapter 5

Nathanial Newberry lived a half-block down Riverfront Street from his parents' mansion. His house was one-third the size, but by today's standards was definitely upper middle class. It was a bungalow with a nice front porch and large high-ceilinged rooms on a lot shaded by large oak trees. The backyard was kept private by a wooden fence that was eight feet high. Several large azalea bushes made the space seem smaller than it actually was. The bushes took up valuable open play area for his two daughters and son Robbie, but made up for it by providing good cover for games of hide-and-seek.

Nate moved into the house believing that one day his family would live in the mansion. After all, Norman and his wife couldn't have kids, Erica was away in another state, and Benji was single. The mansion deserved a family. But a funny thing had happened since he moved into this house almost twelve years ago. He had grown to like it. It was where he and his wife were raising their kids. Although the house would be worth well over $100,000 on the open market, which was more than twice what he had paid for it, the sentimental value to him was much greater. Nathanial Newberry was everything his father was not. The elder Newberry had been gruff and tough, a big man laced with drive and ambition. Nate had become gentle and kind. He had the air of a funeral director, always there to help. Perhaps that was why he was such a good retailer of furniture. Thank goodness his father had started it and then let him take it over.

It was early in the evening when private investigator Jack Boulder called on Nate Newberry. Nate knew right away who the man was at the front door.

"Erica told me that you would be contacting me. Let's go back to the den."

He led Boulder through a hardwood-floored living room and a hallway, then one step down to a large den lined with bookcases on one wall and windows on another that allowed a pleasant view of the backyard. The room was furnished with expensive furniture that was comfortable, but not gaudy. It befit a man who owned a furniture store. Boulder's attention immediately went to a particular piece of furnishing.

"That's a nice gun case you have there," said Boulder.

A woman entered the room. "Jill, this is Jackson Boulder. He's the private detective who Erica hired."

"Pleased to meet you," said Jill, the model of a

soccer mom. Her eyes were red and her hands were quivering. "Can I get you a cup of coffee or something cold to drink?"

"Thank you, I'm fine," Boulder said politely.

She left the room and the two men exchanged a few more pleasantries until Boulder asked Newberry to describe the events of Thanksgiving Day and the hunting accident.

"Thanksgiving morning, my older brother Norm picked up my son Robbie and me here at the house. He already had Benji with him. It was still dark. We drove out to the deer stands. They're on a utility right-of-way that cuts through some family property. We got there right at sunup and took our places on our deer stands and settled in. It was only twenty, maybe thirty minutes, before the first deer appeared. It was a large doe. She walked right down the middle of the line then back into the woods. A few minutes later, a buck appeared, following the same trail as the doe. It looked like a six-pointer, but kind of small. It came from my left and was on the other side of the line. When it got in front of me I fired once and hit him in the rump, I think, because it kicked up a leg and started running to my right, down to where the others were. I heard shots ring out when the deer got down their way."

"How many shots did you hear?" asked Boulder.

"Four, I believe. Maybe more. But I know it was at least three because I thought that Benji, Robbie, and Norm each got a shot."

"Were the shots far apart or close together?"

"Oh, close together. Pop, bam, bam, bam," Newberry said, his voice rising with each shot.

"Pop?"

"Yes. I could tell that Robbie got off the first shot because a four-ten has more of a loud pop to it, while the other guns have a sound like a boom or a bam."

Boulder raised his hand to his chin. "Then what happened?"

"I stayed where I was for a minute, which is what you should do in such a case. Then I saw Norm in the middle of the line waving at me and yelling for me to come there, which I immediately did. He and Robbie were standing there, and he had his arm over Robbie's shoulder. As I walked up, he came to me, put his arm around my shoulder, and turned us away from Robbie. He said that there had been a terrible accident, that Benji had been shot. He said that we should tell Robbie that it was him—that is, Norm—who accidentally shot Benji. Of course, I didn't know what to do. I ran to Robbie and asked him if he was alright, then I went over to where Benji was and saw him laying on the ground. He was already dead."

"Did anyone try to give him CPR?"

"No," said Newberry. "One look and it was obvious that it was too late. Poor Benji."

"Do you really believe that it was Robbie who killed

Benji?" asked Boulder.

Nate Newberry's eyes went down to his hands, which were in his lap, holding onto each other for support. He took a deep breath. "It's been a hard thing to accept. At first I was mad at Norm for placing Benji in a hunting stand directly across from Benji. But Robbie should have known better. Benji was wearing an orange vest. Norm was only trying to protect Robbie. If Robbie ever finds out that he was the one who shot Benji, it will ruin him for life. Robbie is a sensitive boy, Mr. Boulder."

"You didn't answer the question. Do you really believe it was Robbie who killed Benji?"

"I guess so. I think I'm still in a stage of denial that it really happened."

"Do you and Robbie go hunting often?"

"No," said Newberry. "This was Robbie's second or third time in the woods with a gun. I took him dove hunting last fall. The boy seemed to really like it so I decided to take him with us on the Thanksgiving hunt."

"How often do you go hunting?"

He laughed and said, "Once a year."

"At Thanksgiving?"

"Yes. Dad liked to hunt, so all the Newberry boys went hunting on Thanksgiving morning since we were ten years old."

"What about Norm?"

"What about him?"

"Does he hunt often?"

"Norm is the great hunter of the Newberry family. He's even been on a safari in Africa. He would spend every day in the woods hunting if he had his way. You name it and he will hunt it."

The two men sat in silence for a few minutes. Finally, Boulder stood up and walked over to the gun case, which contained several rifles and shotguns, all with orange trigger locks.

"Is Robbie's four-ten in here?"

"Yes. Let me get the key," said Newberry and he left the room.

Boulder looked around at a den that could have been the featured room of the month in a home decorating magazine. It was not too pretentious, but was livable and lovely at the same time. There were plenty of family photographs on the walls and on the tops of end tables.

Soon Newberry returned and opened the gun case. He retrieved the small shotgun and handed it to Boulder. It was a single-shot gun, just like the one Boulder had when he was a boy about Robbie's age. Boulder thought of the squirrel hunts and rabbit hunts his father had taken him on in the woods of central Mississippi not far from Jackson. A four-ten was a good gun for a boy to have as his first gun. He rubbed his hand up and down the barrel and the stock. He broke open the breech and looked down the barrel. He placed his little finger inside the end of the barrel and felt the end of the aiming pin screw that was protruding slightly into the muzzle of the barrel.

"Would you mind if I took this gun for a few days?"

"No. I don't see why not," said Newberry. "Let me get the key to the trigger lock for you."

He went away again and returned in less than a moment with the key. He handed the small shotgun to Boulder, who bid Nathanial Newberry farewell and left with what he hoped was a vital key to who shot Benji Newberry.

Chapter 6

Ethel Newberry was not what Jack Boulder expected. That fact would later cause him an entire night of lost sleep about whether getting older meant more narrow-mindedness and prejudice. But for now he had to deal with what was in front of him

She was not a frail, gray-haired little old lady in her seventies. Instead she stood every bit of five feet eight inches and could have easily been labeled statuesque. Her full head of hair was the color of champagne and was shiny and coiffed. The face surely had the benefit of plastic surgery, for it was smooth and tight. If there was sagging around the neck it was concealed by a multi-colored scarf that went well with the navy blue suit trimmed in gold. The only thing Boulder could detect that might give away her age was the liver spots on the back of her hands that reached out and clasped his in receiving line-like greeting.

"Welcome to my home, Mr. Boulder. Let's go back to the sitting room."

He followed her back to a large sunroom that overlooked an English-style garden that at its rear fell down a bluff to the edge of the river. A maid appeared and in response to Mrs. Newberry's instructions brought them two cups of steaming tea on a silver platter. They performed the ritual of fixing tea, made introductory small talk, and then began the serious part of the conversation.

"So how do you like our little town so far, Mr. Boulder?"

"Unfortunately, I haven't been able to see much of it so far."

"Please be sure to take the Pilgrimage Tour. It's one of the highlights. People come from all over the world to see the beautiful old homes here in Columbus. You would really be amazed at it, I'm sure."

"I don't doubt that for one minute," said Boulder.

"Erica said she was going to hire somebody. She seems to think there may be some hanky-panky going on."

"Why would she think that?"

"Because they all hated Benji," she said matter-offactly, leaving the words to settle in some appropriate place in the room like a set of books with decorative bookends. Boulder did not say anything. "It all came out when Thurston had his heart attack last year and was in the hospital for three weeks. I spent the days at the hospital, and Benji came and spent the nights. He slept in one of those little couch-cots they have nowadays. Norman and Nathanial came by for a few minutes every other day and that was about it."

"What about Erica?"

"She came by the first weekend and then said she needed to get back to the university for final exams. This was last spring."

"How did your husband react to this?"

"At first he was very depressed. He felt like he had been a failure as a father. After all, how would you like to be in the hospital and your own children not come to your side? To him, this proved that he was at fault as a father. I had never seen him cry before then. Shortly after we returned home, he just broke down one night. I talked to the doctor about it and was told that such behavior is not unusual after heart surgery. Anyway, he became obsessed with his death, or should I say the preparation for his death. He called his attorneys and accountants and had them audit the business and make sure everything was in order."

She paused and took a sip of tea. Boulder took the opportunity.

"Is that when he changed his will?"

"Yes."

"In what way?"

"First, let me say that it was not unusual for him to change his will. He had several favorite charities and organizations, and he would amend his will by changing the amounts he left to them. Usually it was an increase. As far as the children were concerned, he had it set up so that they would get equal shares of his remaining assets after his charity, the church, and I were taken care of."

"Can you give me an idea of the amounts, if that's not too personal?"

"The total of the children's share as of last year would probably have amounted to about thirteen million."

Boulder took a breath and a sip of lukewarm tea.

"And how did he change it?" asked Boulder.

"Thurston was watching a television interview one night that featured a nationally known investor who said that wealthy parents who left their fortunes to their children were making a mistake. Thurston starting thinking about his will then. Last August he changed his will so that Norman, Nathanial, and Erica each would receive one hundred thousand dollars plus education costs for any children they might have."

"And Benji?"

"Benji would receive the balance. Thurston felt strongly that all his children except for Benji had abandoned him, and this was his way of punishing them, I guess."

"So Benji would receive over twelve million dollars, and the others would get a hundred thousand apiece?" asked Boulder.

"That's right."

"How did they react when they found out?" asked Boulder, then quickly added, "And how did they find out?"

I'm afraid that's where I come in. I told Thurston that I thought he was making a big mistake. But he was insistent. He believed that the three of them were counting the days until he died." She took a sip of tea. "Oh, that tea has gotten cold. Let me have some more brought in." She picked up a small bell.

"No," said Boulder quickly with an upraised palm. "I'm fine."

"Where was I? Oh, yes. The three of them were just waiting for Thurston to die. Then they began saying things about Benji when they would come over for a visit, which was not very often, I might add. All of this was very distressing to Thurston. I figured that if I told them that their father had changed his will that they would then begin at least acting like they cared for him. That's all he really wanted—for them just to show a little concern. Well, it backfired."

"So when he died, his will left more to Benji than to them."

"Yes," she said. "He had the lawyer come to the house."

"What about the day that he died?"

"It was last Thanksgiving morning. He was sitting in his chair watching television—that's all he did since his heart attack was watch television—when he just laid his head back and sort of grunted. I thought he had gone to sleep and was snoring, but I looked over and saw that the color was gone from his face. I called nine-one-one and told our maid Tessie to go to the front door and watch for the ambulance. The emergency medical people were here in no time, but he was already dead. I instructed Tessie to watch the turkey, and I followed the ambulance to the hospital. I still drive, you know."

"Very impressive."

"They couldn't do anything for Thurston at the hospital, I'm afraid . . . he was already gone. Then I found out about Benji and how he had been shot. I guess you heard what happened to me?"

"No."

"This old body couldn't take it—I fainted. They kept me in a hospital room the rest of the day."

"Mrs. Newberry, this is hard for me to ask, but do you think Benji's death was an accident?"

Her response was firm and immediate. "Of course not. Norman killed him."

Chapter 7

Jack Boulder studied Ethel Newberry. She was sitting tall in the wing-backed chair with both hands on the armrests in the posture of one who is wired up for a lie detector test. In Jack Boulder's experienced police eye she was telling the truth or at least believed that she was telling the truth.

"Why do you think Norman killed Benji?" he asked.

"Please, Mr. Boulder," she said. "Isn't it rather obvious?"

"What about Nathanial? He was there, too. Didn't he have just as much of a motive?"

"Nathanial couldn't kill a fly with a swatter."

"But Norman could?"

"Norman would kill your French poodle if it walked onto his property." They sat there quietly for a moment. Boulder looked out the window at the budding trees. He pictured a fawn walking across the back of the beautifully landscaped lot and its heart being ripped out by a bullet from Norman Newberry's gun. The woman broke the silence. "Mr. Boulder, let me explain my children. Norman, who is the oldest, is a mean, conniving freeloader who never worked a day in his life. All he does is play with guns and ride around in the woods.

"Nathanial is a little better. At least he's a good father to his children. That's more than he got from his father. Nathanial is content to run a furniture store, and if that's what he wants to do, then it's alright with me. I told Thurston that he should have given Nathanial more money, but he wouldn't hear of it. But that's just fine too because when I die Nathanial will get most of what I have. And that's not to be mentioned outside of this room.

"Erica is the real black sheep in the family as far as I'm concerned. She never appreciated the things she had and didn't want to be associated with this family. Do you know that she was married for only a year and still kept her married name? Now that tells me a lot."

"And then there was Benji," said Boulder.

"Benji was a good boy. His brothers mistreated him and played dreadful tricks on him. On the night of his junior-senior prom, they put fish in the back seat of his car during the dance so that when he came out with his date, the car stunk to high heaven."

"I understand that Benji was a good photographer," said Boulder.

"He had a gift in that regard. Would you like to see some of his work?"

"Of course."

They got up and she led him down a long, wide hallway to a more casual room on the other end of the house that also faced the backyard. There were framed photographs lining practically all of the available wall space. The room was a shrine to Benji's photography.

"He took all of these," pronounced Ethel Newberry.

Boulder studied the vast display. The subjects were varied. There was a wall of sunrises and sunsets, a grouping of downtown Columbus buildings, a collection of nature and animal scenes, and a set of bridge photos.

"I'm no photographer, but these are very impressive," said Boulder to the smiling mother. "There are so many different subjects. But I don't see any people in them."

"Oh, there is one," she said and pointed to a spot low on the wall near the hallway door.

Boulder walked over and looked closely. There was a framed eight-by-ten faded color photo, slightly out of focus, that appeared to have been taken with a drugstore camera. The photo depicted a smiling, middle-aged woman in a white Sunday dress sitting in a swing, white-gloved hands in her lap. Boulder looked at the photo, then back to the woman, then to the backyard.

"Why, that's you," remarked Boulder.

"That was Benji's first photograph. The camera was a birthday present when he was nine years old. We had a party in the backyard right after church." There was an odd mixture of pride and melancholy in her voice.

Boulder looked around the room again, this time not paying attention to the photographs on the wall. In one corner was a director's chair where two 35mm cameras lay in its seat. He picked up one and inspected it.

"Those were the cameras Benji had with him on Thanksgiving Day. I just realized that they have been sitting there since then."

Boulder picked up the second camera and immediately noticed a strip of yellow visible through a clear plastic slot on the back of the camera. It was there so that a photographer could see what type film was inside without having to open the camera. In this case it meant that there was still film in the camera.

"Would you mind if I borrowed these cameras for a day or two?"

"I don't see why not," she replied.

Boulder took the cameras by the straps and said farewell to Ethel Newberry. He got in his Camaro and drove downtown to Alford's Drugs on Main Street. It advertised one-hour photo developing. Before going inside, he carefully rewound the film and then opened the camera. He took the film inside and got in a three-person line at the back of the store. He stood patiently, scanning the store, noticing the tin ceiling that must have been there when horses and buggies passed by the front door. Under him was a floor of one-inch black and white tiles. When he got to the front of the line he requested one-hour service; a helpful lady who reminded him of his favorite aunt assured him that it would be no problem.

He walked back out on Main Street, marveling at the traffic. In many downtowns, a person could fire a shotgun on Main Street and not hit anybody. Columbus had figured out how to run a downtown.

Chapter 8

Norman Newberry and his wife Earlene lived in a large house with wood siding that would have been more at home out West than in the middle of the Lowndes County, Mississippi, woods. There was a deep front porch that ran the width of the structure. Six log columns from debarked trees supported a flat, tin roof that protruded over the porch from the main portion of the house. Except for the flavor provided by the columns, the dwelling had all the architectural features of a large shoebox. Behind the house to the left was a metal shed the size of a four-car garage.

Boulder turned the Camaro off the county road onto Newberry's drive and was greeted with a red, black, and white "No Trespassing" sign. He drove a quarter-mile up a narrow, graveled driveway that curved back and forth among tall pines. Even though it was the middle of the afternoon, it suddenly seemed like dusk because the woods were so thick. The road ended in the front yard. He parked beside a new Ford Explorer and got out of his car. From under the front porch he heard a low growl that increased in volume and ferocity as he took three steps forward. Boulder froze. He could not see the dog.

"Shut up, Boomer!" came a harsh voice from around the corner of the house on the side of the metal shed. Norman Newberry appeared and walked forward. "He won't hurt you," he said, then added, "Unless I tell him to."

Newberry stood just over six feet tall and had dark hair and a salt and pepper beard that looked like two-week-old growth. He wore coveralls and a red long-sleeved shirt. His hands hung down and out from his side. Boulder stuck out his hand and said, "I'm Jack Boulder from Jackson."

Newberry raised dirty hands streaked with red liquid and said, "Sorry I can't shake hands. I'm skinning some rabbits. Are you the private eye that Erica hired?" Boulder nodded in the affirmative. "Go on inside and I'll be right in as soon as I clean up."

The front door opened as if in response to his words and a woman appeared.

Without turning, Newberry said, "Earlene, fix Mr. Boulder something to drink."

Boulder walked up the steps and followed Earlene inside as Norman disappeared around the side of the house. Earlene was a redhead in her late forties who was cute in her day, but over the past twenty years had consumed enough biscuits and gravy to add forty extra pounds. She wore tight-fitting blue jeans and a purple sweatshirt that had the word "Falcons" on the front in gold block letters. Her swollen-looking face had no makeup.

"What could I get you to drink, sir? We have Cokes, tea, orange juice, apple juice, milk, and beer."

"I'm fine," said Boulder. "Not a thing."

"Suit yourself."

Boulder scanned the large room and had the feeling he was in a hunting lodge. The large living/dining room looked like a state park cabin. There was a fireplace on the outer wall and at least half a dozen mounted deer heads of trophy size spread throughout.

The front door opened and Norman walked in, wiping his hands with a dark, wet towel. He disappeared through a door, and Boulder heard a refrigerator door open and close, then the sound of a pop and hiss of a can being opened. Norman returned with a can of beer in his hand, and said, "Let's go out on the front porch."

They went outside and took seats in rocking chairs. A warm, southerly wind brushed the treetops.

"It will be raining tomorrow morning," said Norman, scanning what little sky could be seen through the dense trees. "So how can I help you, Boulder?"

"I guess you can tell me about when Benji was shot. Erica says she wants to make sure it was an accident."

"A sad case, I tell you," he said, then took a long swig from the can and burped. "Little Robbie got all excited seeing his first deer and just shot and missed it as it came by. He hit Benji right in the chest. Benji was right across the cut-through."

"The cut-through?"

"Oh. That's what I call those utility right-of-way lines. They just cut through the property. I don't like them because they cut through the woods, but they do provide good hunting opportunities. Are you a hunter?"

"Not since I was a kid," said Boulder. "How far was Robbie from Benji?"

"Couldn't have been more than twenty-five yards. I feel real bad about it. I was the one who placed Robbie there because I didn't want him to feel alone, it being his first deer hunt and all. He was within talking distance of Benji."

"What kind of gun was Robbie using?"

"He had a little four-ten shotgun. He was shooting slugs."

"What kind of gun did Benji have?"

"He had a twelve-gauge shotgun. But Benji wouldn't shoot a rat. He just goes on this hunt every year to humor us."

"I understand that your father changed his will and left quite a bit more money to Benji than to the rest of you," said Boulder.

"That was his prerogative."

"How did that make you feel?"

"You really want to know?"

"Yes," said Boulder.

"I felt sorry for my old man. What he did just proves

that he wasn't in his right mind when he changed his will. He had been acting real strange since he'd had his heart attack. He thought people were out to get him and didn't appreciate him. It was a tough time for him."

"Does that mean that the will is going to be challenged?"

"You can count your cute little car on that," said Newberry firmly.

"I'm not sure I understand what you are saying."

"I've got my lawyer looking into it," said Newberry. "Right now we are all just holding our own until you finish what you're doing."

"Who is 'we'?"

"Look, Boulder, from what I understand you're trying to find out if Benji was killed by accident. These other questions don't have anything to do with that. Understand?"

"What kind of gun were you using that day?"

"My thirty-thirty," said Newberry.

"Do you think it was an accident?"

"That little boy doesn't need to find out he killed a man. He's my nephew. In a way, he's like the son I never had. I'm the one who will take him hunting and fishing. Nate doesn't care for the outdoors. Neither did Benji. A boy needs to get out. Things ought to be left just like they are. It can mess up Robbie if we don't watch out."

"Were you ever in the military?" asked Boulder.

"Special Forces."

"It's time for me to get back to town, Mr. Newberry. I appreciate your talking to me."

"Yeah, sure."

Boulder got back in his car and returned to town. He went first to the Amzi Love House, where he was greeted by Katherine with a message. "Laura called and said to tell you that she was in federal court in Oxford today and will come through Columbus early tonight. She said she would meet you here at six o'clock."

The news warmed Boulder. He was ready to tell her about this case and get her opinion. He was also ready for Laura's company. The case had taken his mind off his increasing feelings for her, but he was ready for what was in his heart to resume.

Feeling joyous at this news, he almost forgot that he had photos to pick up at the drugstore. He drove back downtown and picked up what was surely the last roll of film taken by Benji Newberry. He sat down in his car and eagerly opened the envelope. There were a dozen color prints of squirrels, birds, and naked tree limbs against the sky. Boulder couldn't be sure, but it appeared that the pictures were taken from the hunting stand where Benji was on Thanksgiving morning. The last three photographs caused Boulder's stomach to tighten. The first of the three showed Robbie sitting down beside a tree, his shotgun held across his chest. An eleven-year-old boy in the woods. The second shot depicted Norman approximately twenty-five feet away in hunter orange inspecting a large silver revolver in his hands. The last print was a closer view of Norman, as if the lens had zoomed in. The pistol was now pointed straight at the camera.

Chapter 9

Laura Webster arrived in Columbus shortly before six o'clock p.m. They decided to go to Ruben's and have catfish. The restaurant was located close to downtown on the riverfront and had walkways out back so that boaters could dock and come in for dinner. Like any good catfish house, Ruben's had oilcloth-covered tables in every size, from tables that seated two to tables that seated twenty. Near the front was a floor-to-ceiling log that had been cut in such a way that the limbs stuck out a few inches, making it an excellent, if unorthodox, hat rack. The ceiling was low and there was what appeared to be mud in the light fixtures, but the view to the river was excellent. They were seated promptly and in a few minutes were munching away on fried catfish, hush-puppies, and all the other trimmings appropriate to such a meal.

"Where are you folks from?"

It was a female voice from a couple sitting next to

them. They looked to be in their early sixties, dressed casually, and had year-round tans.

"We're from Jackson," said Laura. "How about you?"

"Ohio," the woman replied.

"I should have said Jackson, Mississippi, then."

"We're here for the Pilgrimage, but we're running way ahead of schedule, so we're a few days early. We travel by boat."

Boulder and Laura instinctively looked out at the river. There were two houseboats and a large cabin cruiser in view.

"Let me guess," said Boulder. "The one on the right."

"You got it."

They learned that the MacDonalds were traveling down the Tennessee-Tombigbee on their cruiser and planned to go all the way to Mobile. They were retired and spent three to four months each year on their boat. They had a second home in Ft. Lauderdale and would probably leave their boat there. They were excited about the Pilgrimage, but were unable to glean any information from the Jackson couple because neither of them had ever been to the event. When the MacDonalds' order arrived they broke off the conversation and turned to their dining. Boulder got down to business about his case in Columbus.

Boulder took a sip of iced tea and began. He gave Laura the background about the change in the will, then talked about the results of his interviews regarding the accident itself.

"I'll state the facts, as I know them. Thurston Newberry has a heart attack and is taken to the hospital where he is pronounced dead by the attending physician. His youngest son, Benji, is shot sometime that same morning while hunting with his brothers and is taken to the same hospital where he is pronounced dead by the same physician. In the emergency room, the brothers inform the doctor that Benji was actually shot by Robbie, who is the son of Nathanial—the middle brother—but they do not want Robbie to know that he did the shooting. Norman acts as if he fired the shot that killed Benji. The doctor calls the coroner, who comes to the emergency room, looks at the body, and interviews the brothers. The coroner sees no need for an autopsy because the death is an accident, and Benji is later buried with the slug that killed him still inside of him." He paused a moment, then said, "Are you thoroughly confused now?"

"I think I've got it," said Laura. "I have some questions, but I'll save them for later. Go on."

"I interview brother Nathanial, the father of Robbie. He confirms the incident, but he was not in place to see who actually did the shooting. He let me borrow the four-ten. I want to have some ballistics tests done on it."

"Why?"

"I noticed that the aiming pin at the end of the barrel has protruded inside the barrel. It's possible that it puts a mark on any shots that are fired through the barrel."

"I thought that shotguns couldn't be matched with a specific shell."

"That's true if the shell contained pellets—those little BBs. But if a large piece of lead, called a slug, is shot through the barrel, it would be possible that it is marked by the little screw of the aiming pin. There would be no grooves on the slug like on a rifle, because a shotgun doesn't have grooves. But if we did a ballistics test and found that this shotgun left a groove on the slug, then it would be possible to compare it to the slug that killed Benji."

"Which is still inside the body," pointed out Laura.

"Right," said Boulder. "But let me add two other pieces of evidence. First, and I admit that this might not be very good evidence, but the mother says that Nathanial didn't have the guts to kill somebody; and she believes that Norman killed Benji. I interviewed Norman this afternoon. He is certifiably creepy and lives in the woods and hunts all the time. He knows firearms backwards and forward. But here's the coup de grâce: The last photo on Benji's roll of film is of Norman in the woods pointing a pistol right at him."

"So what's your next move?" asked Laura.

"I'm going to have that ballistics test done at the state crime lab if possible, then go to the district attorney. I'm afraid we need to look at the slug in Benji's body. If Robbie's shotgun makes a groove when a slug is shot through it, and if there is not a groove on the slug in Benji's body, we then know that Robbie's gun didn't kill him."

"Do you think Norman killed him?"

"He would be the likely suspect," said Boulder. "He had a motive because he was cut out of an inheritance. He had the opportunity because he was at the site. He also had the means."

"Explain that part," said Laura.

"In the last two photographs in the film, he is seen with a pistol—a chrome-plated or stainless steel revolver. It was bigger than a standard thirty-eight. I think it might be a forty-four magnum."

"Keep going."

"A forty-four magnum would make an entry wound about the same size as that of a four-ten slug," said Boulder.

"So an attending physician would not suspect because the wound matched the story of the witnesses?"

"That's right."

A server approached their table and took their plates. She recited the dessert list. They each opted for coffee and pecan pie.

"Do you remember that once upon a time you and I rented a Dirty Harry movie?" asked Boulder. "He carried a forty-four magnum, the world's most powerful handgun."

"If the movie was correct and if Norman Newberry

used a forty-four magnum, wouldn't it have blown Benji back and maybe even gone right through him?" asked Laura.

"Depending on the bullet, it would have probably gone in the size of a dime and come out the size of a baseball if it were a forty-four magnum," he said.

"Seems like a good defense lawyer would point that out?"

"Unless it could be shown that Norman loaded the ammunition himself with a smaller amount of powder."

"And how could that be proven?"

"It might be hard," said Boulder. "But Norman is a real outdoorsman. It would be interesting to know what is inside that outbuilding beside the house."

"You might not want to know," said Laura.

"You know what? I think I'll just do that ballistics test myself. I can do it this weekend and if it's a slug with a gouge mark in it I'll be in the district attorney's office Monday morning."

"That sounds like a plan," said Laura. Boulder smiled. She looked good tonight.

"Laura, can I talk to you about something else?" asked Boulder, his palms beginning to sweat.

"Of course," she said with a smile. "But first I have a question and an observation."

"Go right ahead."

"Do you know who died first? The father or the son?"

"The father was pronounced dead first," said Boulder.

"But did he actually die first?" she asked.

"I don't know if that's been looked at very closely," said Boulder. "Even if it were, it might be very difficult to ascertain. Is that important?"

"It might be," said Laura. "If Thurston Newberry died first, then this will you keep referring to would go into effect. Benji's estate would be the beneficiary and would receive Thurston's money as provided for in the will."

"Wouldn't the death certificate show who died first?" asked Boulder, already planning a trip to the Bureau of Vital Statistics.

"The death certificate carries the time that the emergency room physician pronounces him dead, after all life-saving efforts have been exhausted. So the certificate might not show you what you need."

"And if Benji died first?"

"If Benji died first then neither he nor his estate could be the beneficiary, assuming that the standard clauses are in the will. The will would be probated and the chances are good that the previous will would stand. It would be up to the chancellor to decide."

"So if Benji died first, the other three would get all the money he planned to give Benji? A hundred thousand versus millions."

"That's right."

"Now we have revenge and lots of money as a motive."

Chapter 10

Boulder and Laura stayed the night in Columbus. He never got around to asking her the other question he had in mind. The possibility of time of death being an issue in the case dominated the remainder of their conversation. On Friday they followed each other back to Jackson, she in her Jaguar and he in his Camaro. Boulder decided that it would be better to talk about the future with Laura after this case was concluded.

He took the shotgun to a retired state trooper friend's house in the country. They set up a plastic barrel filled with water and shot twelve slugs into it from the gun. Every slug had a straight groove mark in it. Now it was possible to prove that the slug in Benji's body either came from this gun or not. Boulder's enthusiasm for this case was growing.

On Sunday he drove back to Columbus and checked in at the Amzi Love House once again.

Early Monday morning he went to the courthouse annex and found the district attorney's office. The receptionist looked at him suspiciously when he asked to talk to the district attorney.

"May I ask what it is in reference to?" the receptionist asked.

"Could you just say that it is regarding a criminal matter?"

She had heard this statement over a hundred times, and she knew exactly what to do. She phoned the youngest, newest assistant on the staff and said that there was a walk-in who wanted to discuss a criminal case. Boulder was then ushered into a small office where a serious-looking woman in her mid-twenties was sitting behind a desk using a yellow Highlighter pen on a legal brief. She didn't get up. He sat down.

Assistant District Attorney Marcia Stockwell was an earnest woman, serious about her first job after graduation from Ole Miss Law School. She had been here for nine months now, handling increasingly complex cases under the tutoring eyes of the district attorney, but also handling the walk-ins. She wore a gray suit trimmed in darker gray, her outfit resembling a plebe uniform at a military academy. Her hair was dark and straight and short. The sternness on her face was exceeded only by the rigidity of her body. She was an ideal public servant, married to her job.

"How can I help you?"

He introduced himself and handed her one of his cards. She put her elbows on her cluttered desk and listened patiently as he detailed his investigation to date.

He left out the part about his amateur ballistics test.

"That's very interesting, but it sounds like more of a civil case," she said.

"That's what I thought you might say." He reached in his pocket and laid a plastic freezer bag containing twelve slugs on her desk. She picked it up and began studying the pieces of lead. "Notice anything similar about those slugs?"

"They each have a little nick in them," she said.

"What made that nick was the end of the screw on the aiming pin of the boy's shotgun. If that shotgun killed Benji Newberry, then the slug that killed him would match those grooves."

"Do you have that slug?"

"No."

"And where might it be?" she asked. Boulder smiled like a cat with feathers around its mouth. "Oh, I get it. Don't tell me. Let me guess. It's still inside the body, isn't it?"

"That is correct," said Boulder.

"You're not going to ask what I'm thinking you're about to ask."

"I am."

"Exhuming a body is a serious matter, Mr. . . . ."

"Boulder."

"Mr. Boulder."

"As serious as murder," he said.

She leaned back and looked at the ceiling as she

processed the information before her. She leaned forward and said, "What if the slugs don't match?"

"Then it looks like you've got a murder case on your hands."

She turned around and reached into the bookcase behind her and retrieved a blue-bound volume of the Mississippi Code. She opened it, flipped a few pages, then read intensely for a moment. She addressed Boulder in the manner of a law professor lecturing a class.

"There are two alternatives in such a case. If there is sufficient cause for further investigation after a body has been buried, then the medical examiner shall authorize an investigation and send a report with a recommendation to the district attorney. The district attorney then forwards the report to the circuit court with a petition for disinterment. Then the circuit judge may order that the body be exhumed and an autopsy performed by the state medical examiner. However, the state medical examiner is able to authorize disinterment if there is a suspicion of homicide."

"Sounds like that applies to this case," said Boulder.

"The other alternative is that any individual may petition the circuit court for an exhumation order," she added.

"What do you think we should do?"

"Is there a risk of flight by the suspect?" she asked.

"How should I know?" said Boulder. "He has been a member of this community all his life."

"If we call the state medical examiner, it's going to make our local coroner feel slighted even though he did exactly the right thing under the circumstances." She picked up the telephone and instructed the receptionist to page the coroner to come to her office.

An hour later the three of them sat in the conference room and reviewed the case. Soon a petition was filed with the court, and an order was issued authorizing the disinterment of the body of Benjamin Whitby Newberry.

Chapter 11

Friendship Cemetery is located about a mile south of downtown Columbus on a bluff overlooking the Tombigbee River. It is listed on the National Register of Historic Places. It was begun on May 30, 1849, and contains the remains of four Congressmen, two Mississippi governors, several Mississippi University for Women presidents, five generals of the Confederate States of America, hundreds of soldiers of various wars, and hundreds of citizens who called the area home and chose this spot as their final resting place. It is probably most well-known as the site of the first Decoration Day, which is now observed as Memorial Day in the United States. On April 25, 1866, four Columbus women decorated the graves of both Union and Confederate soldiers in a show of impartiality to either side. Their act was immortalized in a poem entitled "The Blue and Gray," which appeared in the September 1867 edition of *The Atlantic Monthly*.

Jack Boulder got up at six o'clock on Wednesday morning and decided that he would jog down to Friendship Cemetery for his morning run. He wanted to reconnoiter the area prior to the disinterment of Benji Newberry later that morning. He consulted a local brochure and saw that he needed only to go over a few blocks and then down Fourth Street to the cemetery. He headed out in shorts and a jogging suit jacket to protect against the cool, damp air of the morning. When he got to the cemetery, he did a long lap around it and then began walking along the lanes that were named for various flowers—Hackberry, Magnolia, Dogwood, White Oak, Elm, and more. He walked up to the Decoration Day monument and was immediately struck by the uniform starkness of the hundreds of cross-shaped markers that read simply, "An Unknown Confederate Soldier." Below and behind the monument he could see the river and the milky fog rising gently upward from it like dry ice.

He began reading tombstones and noticed that the tombstones for the men provided brief information, while those for women contained much more description of the person. He stooped down and read the headstone of a woman who was buried in June of 1876:

> *Her heart was the playground*
> *of all human Charities, they met and reveled there; and*
> *then went forth in search of pain, and want, and suffering.*
> *The Cross. Now the crown.*

He took time to read another one twice because of its beauty and expression:

> *Just as the last rays of sun kissed the earth,*
> *her dear spirit took its flight to that happy land*
> *where the wings of the soul are unfurled.*
> *My own beloved, darling wife, Thou art called first,*
> *the cord which unites us is not broken.*
> *It will not suffer hurt by the desolation and wreck*
> *of death, but will live on, with undisturbed*
> *vigor, freshness and beauty in the midst*
> *of decay.*

The words made him start thinking of his girlfriend Laura. There had been a change in him recently when it came to her. Maybe he was facing his mid-life crisis. He felt he wanted something he had never really wanted before. Did he want a permanent relationship?

He walked on into the cemetery, now off the paved lanes and onto the ground between the graves. It seemed like there were a lot of people buried here who were born in Georgia and South Carolina. He also noticed that it was easy to find the graves of the little children. Just look for a lamb on the headstone. The most notable headstone was the obelisk, which resembled the Washington Monument. There were also lots of Woodmen of the World tombstones in the shapes of tree trunks and logs. Was it his imagination, or were there more angel headstones in this cemetery? How would he know? He had never been a cemetery aficionado.

In the center of Friendship Cemetery were two huge magnolia trees, so large that a husband and wife could not wrap their arms around either trunk. Boulder walked over to one of the trees and walked slowly and deliberately out from the trunk to the end of the branches. Fourteen paces. Nearby was a white gazebo with a green shingled roof. He walked slowly toward it, sat down on the bench inside of it, closed his eyes and inhaled slowly.

"Did you see the angel?"

Boulder jerked forward, startled. In front of him were two teenage boys in jeans and jackets. He looked around slowly and saw a red Honda Civic that had not been there before.

"We're sorry," said one. "We didn't mean to make you jump."

"No problem," said Boulder. "Mind if I ask what you're doing in a cemetery at six-thirty in the morning?"

"We're getting into our parts," said the other. "During the Pilgrimage, we'll be down here for *Tales From The Crypt,* and we have do a little more research on our characters."

"What's *Tales From The Crypt?*"

"It's part of the Columbus Pilgrimage. One of the tours is of this cemetery. We go to high school at M-S-M-S, that's Mississippi School for Math and Science, and one of our history projects is to learn about some-one buried here. The Pilgrimage has candlelight tours through here, and we students stand by the graves of our person we researched and give a monologue about his or her life."

"We even have to wear the clothes like that person would have worn," said the other student.

"You're kidding," said Boulder. "That's neat."

"Last year, over a thousand people came through."

"You asked if I had seen the angel?" said Boulder.

"Follow us."

They led him a short distance to a large tombstone with just a last name engraved on it. Leaning over the tombstone was an almost life-sized angel, with its head lying on the top of the tombstone. It was a work of art.

"Look at the eyes," said one of the students.

Boulder bent forward. "It's crying."

"They say that the angel is crying because the man in the grave was so good to everybody in the community that when he died even the angels cried.

"Let's show him Miss Munroe!"

They led him even farther to a large brick monument that looked like a small room. The top of it was at least twelve feet from the ground. It had all the trappings of a mausoleum.

"This is where we bring our dates when we really want to frighten them. We pull up beside Miss Munroe's grave and say, 'Miss Munroe, Miss Munroe, Is there anything we can bring you?' Then from inside comes a voice that says 'Nothing at all."

Boulder grinned at their enthusiasm and said, "Any other noteworthy graves?"

"There are many. But I like Orphan Annie," said one of the boys. "It's just a plain marker in the ground that

reads Annie. She was some orphan that everybody liked and didn't have a grave marker when she died, so someone paid for that one."

Boulder glanced at his digital watch and said, "I better get going. Thanks for the information."

"Don't forget—*Tales From The Crypt!*"

Boulder assured him that he would come back during Pilgrimage, then he jogged back to the Amzi Love House, had breakfast, put on fresh clothes, and returned to Friendship Cemetery.

At nine o'clock a.m. a collection of people gathered at the gravesite in Friendship Cemetery. The assemblage included, among others, the county medical examiner, Assistant District Attorney Stockwell, a deputy sheriff, the previous funeral director, Jack Boulder, and the two gravediggers who had dug the original grave. A crowd of onlookers had formed at the entrance to the cemetery as a result of a front-page article that appeared in the *Columbus Packet,* a local alternative newspaper. The newspaper article contained the entire court petition, verbatim. The newspaper wondered editorially if murder had paid a visit to one of the town's most prominent families.

The unearthing and removal of the casket took less than thirty minutes. It was placed in the back of the hearse and by agreement of the officials involved, transported to the funeral home, where the group reconvened. It took an even shorter time to open the casket and remove the slug from the body. The medical examiner laid the piece of lead on the embalming table. The assistant district attorney laid Boulder's plastic bag of slugs next to it. The two items were examined and compared.

"It is obvious that the slug retrieved from the body is different from the slug provided by Mr. Boulder," announced the medical examiner. "It appears therefore that the shot that caused the death of Benjamin Newberry was not fired from the shotgun in the possession of Robbie Newberry on the day of the incident. However, let us not jump to conclusions. A complete autopsy will be performed before the body is returned to the grave."

That was the signal most of them wanted so that they could leave before the autopsy began. While the autopsy was being performed, word spread quickly around town that Benji Newberry had been murdered. Along with the rumor went speculation as to which brother had killed the youngest brother. One person even opined that it was actually a suicide.

At five o'clock that afternoon, Boulder and Stockwell sat in her office reviewing Boulder's information in detail. Stockwell was already mentally preparing for her first murder case. As they were talking, the receptionist stuck her head in the door and said, "I thought you might want to know that the Sheriff's Office is sending a car to Norman Newberry's home."

Marcia Stockwell clenched her teeth, banged her fist on her desk, and stood up.

"What are they doing? We haven't had a warrant issued yet or even talked about presenting it to a grand jury," she fumed. Boulder leaned back. This little lawyer had spunk. It was time for his violet to be shrinking.

"I'm sorry," said the receptionist. "They are responding to a telephone call from Mrs. Earlene Newberry, who said that her husband had killed himself."

"Oh."

"I'll be going home now," said the receptionist.

Chapter 12

Jack Boulder jumped up and headed for the door.

"Come on. Let's go," he shouted at Marcia Stockwell. Confusion plastered itself on her face. "I'll explain on the way."

They walked down the narrow hallway and bounded down the metal steps of the courthouse annex to Boulder's Camaro, which was parked on Lawyers' Row. They jumped in and he sped away toward a county road that led to the long driveway of Norman Newberry's house.

"What is the big rush, may I ask?" as Boulder shifted into fourth gear and accelerated away from downtown.

"How many homicides has the Sheriff's Department worked in the last five years?" asked Boulder.

"How would I know? I've only been here nine months. I grew up in Gulfport."

"Okay. How many in nine months?"

"I don't know," she replied. "Maybe four or five. Columbus is not exactly the crime capital of the United States. Watch that log truck! It's about to make a turn."

"With all due respect, I worked that many homicides every month in St. Louis," said Boulder.

"What's your point?"

"We need to have a crime scene that is undisturbed."

"This is a suicide," she practically shouted. "Would you please slow down!"

"That's the point. If they go in and treat it like a suicide instead of a homicide they might contaminate valuable evidence that you need in a trial later on."

"I see your point," she said. "Hurry up!"

Boulder's best imitation of a Dukes of Hazzard country road driving scene was rewarded by being third on the scene after a deputy sheriff and the ambulance. As he and Stockwell got out of the car, they heard the sound of distant electronic yelping sirens. It was about to be a madhouse around the place. The door to the metal shed was halfway open, and Boulder caught sight of the deputy's shirt sleeve. He walked quickly to the

82

building, Stockwell doing her best to keep up. As he approached, the deputy, looking every bit like he graduated from high school within the past three years, raised his palm.

"Sorry, sir. You can't go in here."

"Who's in there now?" demanded Boulder.

The deputy did not reply; however, he recognized Marcia Stockwell as an assistant district attorney when she approached. "Hello, ma'am."

"Who's inside?" she asked, as Boulder attempted to peer over his shoulder.

"Two EMT's are checking the body for signs of life. I told them not to disturb anything because we need to preserve the scene for the criminal investigator. I'll have some crime scene tape around the whole building when my backup gets here."

Stockwell looked at Boulder and gave him a "How do you feel now?" look. He read it perfectly and said, "I apologize." Turning to the deputy he said, "YOU did a good job, Deputy. How did you know that crime scene preservation was so important?"

"I just graduated from the state law enforcement academy, sir."

Forty-five minutes later the coroner was on the scene, and Boulder and Stockwell were finally allowed to go inside the shed.

Norman Newberry's body was in a chair and slumped forward over a marble-covered table on which there were several small boxes of gunpowder, shell casings, and other ammunition reloading paraphernalia. Lying on the tabletop, four inches from his right hand, was a pearl-handled, stainless steel Smith & Wesson revolver. Boulder leaned down and looked closely at the pistol. He then walked slowly around the body. There was a maroon-colored dark spot on the left side of the head directly above the ear. Boulder backed two steps away from the chair, raised his hand, and pointed his right index finger at where Newberry's head would have been if he were working at the table. The coroner, Stockwell, and the sheriff's criminal investigator watched transfixed as Boulder did his work. Boulder backed up to the door of the shed, walked up to the chair, and raised his hand again. He then moved around behind the chair, leaned down to the corner of the marbletop table, and, making sure not to touch it, pointed to a nick in the tabletop. He then followed an imaginary line from the nick upwards at a forty-five degree angle to a spot in a wood two-by-four wall brace. He pointed his finger to within an inch of the brace and motioned for the sheriff's investigator, who walked over and stood beside Boulder.

"Looks like a twenty-two," he said.

They backed away from the wall and Boulder began.

"I don't want to jump to conclusions because there is still a lot of work to be done here, but it appears that the perpetrator came in and shot Newberry in the side of the head with a twenty-two caliber rifle or pistol. Since we

84

have all walked or driven over the yard and driveway, we have probably destroyed any physical evidence, such as footprints, that would be useful. It is noted that the revolver on the table is a Smith and Wesson forty-one caliber, which just happens to fire the same size round as a four-ten shotgun. Given Mr. Newberry's talents as an expert shooter, and now learning that he reloads ammunition as well, I suspect that we might find that the bullet in Benji's body came from this gun. It is reasonable to believe that Norman had the ability to put together a shell casing, powder, and lead round that would mimic a four-ten shotgun slug."

They all stood still, processing what Boulder just said.

"So you think this is not a suicide?" said Marcia Stockwell.

"Take a look at the entry point right above the ear," said Boulder. "I'll bet the exit wound is in front of the other ear."

The coroner walked over to the body and with latex-gloved hands gently lifted the head. He looked at Stockwell and nodded in the affirmative.

"That means someone was beside him and just slightly behind. It was probably someone he knew, because the shot appears to have been fired while he was looking forward and down at his work on the table. That is not exactly the position someone would be in if he was threatened. Obviously, he didn't use the forty-one Smith and Wesson. It would have taken his head off. Which brings us to the next question."

"Where's the gun?" It was Marcia Stockwell.

"Deputy, do you know who made this call?" asked Boulder.

"I understand it was Mrs. Newberry. She's inside the house with a female deputy."

"I think she needs to be asked why she reported this as a suicide," said Boulder.

The voice of Earlene Newberry came from the doorway behind them.

"I did not kill my husband," she said slowly and deliberately with a slight quiver. "But I can tell you who did."

Chapter 13

The sheriff's criminal investigator stepped forward and took over.

"Mrs. Newberry, you are advised that you have the right to remain silent. You have the right to an attorney before answering any questions. If you start answering any questions, you have the right to stop answering questions at any time. If you cannot afford an attorney, one will be appointed for you. Do you understand these rights?"

"I do."

"Do you wish to make a statement at this time?"

"Yes."

"Just a minute," said Marcia Stockwell. "I suggest we leave here and go to the conference room at the courthouse."

"I think I would prefer that," said Earlene Newberry. She raised up on tiptoes and looked toward the body of her husband. "Is Norman dead?"

"I'm afraid so," said Stockwell.

Earlene Newberry and the assistant district attorney got in the back of the criminal investigator's black, unmarked Crowne Victoria and rode downtown. Earlene was interviewed in a conference room at the courthouse and would later place her signature on a typed statement.

Meanwhile, Boulder stayed behind and observed the collection of evidence and photographic documentation of the crime scene. He didn't want any mistakes. He had witnessed too many contaminated crime scenes in St. Louis, where eager or inexperienced police officers or medical examiners handled evidence improperly.

He took a moment to scan the large metal outbuilding. The interior resembled a cross between a gun manufacturing operation and the hunting and fishing section of a sporting goods store.

Later, he drove back downtown to Stockwell's office. She handed him the signed statement of Earlene Newberry.

At approximately 4:00 p.m. today I answered a tele-phone call at home from my brother-in-law, Nathanial Newberry. He asked to speak to my husband Norman, who is also his brother. I gave the telephone to my husband and went into another room. I heard him exclaim loudly, "What!" and then about three minutes of conversation that I could not hear very well. Then I heard my husband say, "You don't have the guts" in a mean voice. Then he hung up the phone.

About twenty minutes later, Nate showed up at our house. He came to the front door and asked for Norman. I told him that Norman was in the shed. Nate went to the shed and from the porch, I heard them arguing in loud voices, but I could not understand what they were saying. They stopped arguing for a few minutes, then I heard a gunshot like a .22 or a pellet gun. It was a loud crack.

I went back inside the house. Nate came inside and told me to call the sheriff and say that Norman's death was a suicide. Then I would get a lot of money. So I did as I was told.

/s/ Earlene Newberry

Chapter 14

It was now 8:45 p.m. and Jack Boulder and Marcia Stockwell were in the courthouse conference room waiting for news from the sheriff's department, which was attempting to serve an arrest warrant on Nathanial Newberry.

Deputies had gone to Newberry's home only to be told by a frantic wife that her husband did not come home from work at six o'clock that evening, as was his normal practice. He had never come home late before, she told them. Ethel Newberry, the mother, said that she would call the police if she heard anything from her son.

Little did they know that at this very moment Nathanial Newberry was sitting in the middle of the old river bridge attempting to get drunk on a bottle of bourbon he had purchased earlier. He would take a huge swallow, then another, then throw up in the river below. His life was coming unraveled, and he did not know what to do. All he could think of was to come to the river, the place of so many boyhood memories. Below him was Riverside Park, where he first kissed the girl who would later become his wife. Farther down the river about a mile was a spot where he and his boyhood pals had set out trot lines and camped all night.

Yes, the river had been a part of his early life, and maybe now it would wash all his sins away. He would get drunk and fling himself to waters far below to be swept up in the redemption of death. But he knew better. If he jumped he would not die. He had leaped from this very bridge when he was thirteen years old, when his friends had called him "chicken" and "yellow" and "sissy." He had fought back the tears and the fear of falling and had jumped! He had hit the water feet first and thought he was going to drown when the water went up his nose. But he did not succumb to the river. He emerged to the cheers of his so-called friends, who now accepted him as one of them. To Nate Newberry it was a day secretly more important than getting married or being present for his first-born child's birth. The day he jumped off the old river bridge was the day he became a man. And now he was about to do it again. And what would he become this time?

He took another drink—this time, only one sip—and found that he did not feel as nauseous. He discovered

that by drinking small amounts he could keep the burning liquid down. Tears filled his eyes and he began sobbing. What had life become? His older brother had killed his younger brother. And he had killed his older brother.

He felt a mixture of every painful emotion he had ever experienced in his life. He had yet to mourn the death of his brother Benji because he had been consumed with concern over his son Robbie.

This afternoon, he had learned from an employee— an employee!—that Norman was the one who had killed Benji. He went into a silent rage. How could Norman have killed Benji, and blamed it on Robbie? What vile, evil man could do such a thing to his family? Nate could not allow such a thing as had been done to his son to go unpunished. To make sure that it was true, he had called Norman first and confronted him with what he had heard about the slugs. He threatened to kill Norman, to which his older brother responded that he did not have the guts. So he had taken the little twenty-two caliber pistol from his desk drawer at the furniture store and gone to see his older brother, who told him that he was stupid. With Benji out of the way, they would get the money. Norman finally said, "If you are going to kill me, make it look like a suicide or else your family won't get any money." Norman had dared him. Just like the boys who had dared him to jump off the bridge, knowing he couldn't do it. And like the other boys, Norman found out that

Nate wasn't such a chicken after all. Norman had turned his head back to putting bullets together, and Nate pulled out his little gun and put a bullet in his head. On the way out he had told Norman's wife to say it was a suicide, or she would not get any money. It was all he could think of to say at the time.

Now the alcohol was doing its job. Nathanial Newberry crawled over to the edge, braced himself on one of the metal spans, and stood up. With tears streaming down his face, and a heart full of pain, and dizziness overtaking his brain, he lay back down on the bridge and fell sound asleep in the cold March air.

Chapter 15

Nathanial Newberry was found the next morning by the MacDonalds, the river-cruising tourist couple from Ohio who were out on an early morning walk down by the riverfront. At first they thought they had discovered a dead body on the bridge.

Newberry was taken to the hospital with a mild case of exposure. A deputy was posted outside his room. His wife was smart enough to hire a lawyer, who called the district attorney's office and informed them that Newberry would not be making any statements to the authorities. Jack Boulder arrived at Marcia Stockwell's office at 8:30 a.m. and was told the news.

"Quite a dysfunctional family," remarked Stockwell.

"No doubt about that," agreed Boulder as he sipped coffee from a courthouse styrofoam cup. "But I doubt that there are many families that would not come apart in the same situation. The money is one thing, but jealousy is a powerful motivator, especially when it comes to brothers and sisters."

"You sound philosophical."

"I guess I've just seen too many victims of jealousy and greed."

"How many homicides would you say you have worked in your career?" she asked.

He did the mental math and said, "Somewhere in the neighborhood of seven hundred."

"My gosh!"

"That's just one a week for fourteen years if my arithmetic is correct. I took off two weeks each year for vacation. Most were drug-related or somebody getting drunk and shooting somebody else over some little dispute that triggered the rage."

"How many went to court?"

"Only a very few," he said. "Most of the defendants pleaded guilty to manslaughter. I would say that an average of only three a year went right down to a Perry Mason trial where there was testimony."

"Got any tips for a young prosecutor?"

"Verify everything," he said without hesitation.

"Witnesses, including law enforcement personnel, will tell you what they think you want to hear, not what they actually remember. I've seen too many cases where witnesses actually believed something to be true when it was inconclusively proven false. That's where the prosecutor really looks stupid. And I mean verify everything, no matter how small or insignificant it might seem."

"That's good advice," she said. "I'll remember it."

"Got any tips for a private eye?"

"You already know more than most people will ever learn about your business."

"Got any advice for the opposite sex?"

"What do you mean?"

"What advice would you give to someone who said he would never get married again and now wants to get married?" asked Boulder.

"Would marriage draw her closer or push her farther away?"

"Good question," said Boulder.

"Nowadays, women have choices," she said. "Some of them don't want to choose, though. They want both —a marriage and a career."

"Hmm."

"What kind of career does this woman have?"

"She's a lawyer."

"Oh, wow," she grinned. "You are really in trouble."

"Really?"

"Women lawyers either want both, or they want the law," she said.

"You sound very confident for a female lawyer who has been practicing for less than a year," he said.

"We talked a lot about this subject in law school. And every time a female guest lecturer came in we asked her opinion. It was unanimous. Once a woman becomes passionate for the law, it will always be there."

"But there's room for both, you say?"

"Yes," she replied. "Just don't ask her to give up the law for marriage."

"I'll keep that in mind."

"Are you heading back to Jackson now?"

"Later today," he said. "I'd like to stroll around downtown for a while. This is really one of the best downtowns I have ever seen."

"I'll be calling you to testify if we go to trial with Nathanial Newberry," she said.

"I will be available," said Boulder. "I turned the shotgun over to the sheriff's department. Don't forget chain of custody. Also, if it goes to trial you will probably want the state crime lab to do another ballistics test on the gun."

"I'll keep that in mind."

"I would not look for this one to go to trial, though. He's probably going to plead temporary insanity. A good defense lawyer could throw a lot of curves. Earlene Newberry's statement would probably be thrown out. A wife still can't testify against her husband, I don't think. On the other hand, a good prosecutor would tear them apart."

"Good-bye, Jack Boulder."

He left and began his downtown stroll. Before long he had made his way almost to the riverfront when he was approached by an enthusiastic, but eccentric looking man in his mid-fifties.

"Hello," said the man. "You're new around here, aren't you?"

"Yes," said Boulder.

"Tourist or new resident?"

"I'm here on business. Today is my last day in town."

"I'm Harry Ludlam. Better known as the Sidewalk Superintendent of Columbus." His hand was outstretched. "Pleased to meet you. Have you gotten the weather update today?"

"No. Can't say that I have."

"Chance of rain for tomorrow. There will be a front coming in. If it's slow there will be a good sunset on River Hill tonight. High thin clouds over the prairie make for exceptional sunsets here," said the man.

"I appreciate that information, but I'll be gone by then," said Boulder.

"Oh, I don't think so," said Harry. "You haven't finished your investigation."

Chapter 16

Harry Ludlam led Jack Boulder down Main Street, stopping several times to pick up gum wrappers, pieces of metal, stray pieces of paper, and even a bird feather. He called them his little treasures. Ludlam, once known as a brilliant city planner in a large city out West, had suffered a serious concussion in an automobile accident a few years ago. Unable to work in his chosen profession any longer, he moved back to his boyhood home of Columbus and took it upon himself to make the community a better place. To Harry Ludlam, a community could not be at its best if it was not at its cleanest. Aesthetics defined a community and to Harry beauty in Columbus started with clean streets and ended with beautiful sunsets. Some of the "treasures" he discovered on the streets were used in creations tucked away in his house and known only to a few. Every day Harry got up early and began his rounds in downtown Columbus and in the residential area on the south side of town. He stopped in for coffee at will at any number of businesses. Some say he was tolerated; most say he was cherished.

They walked on in the downtown area. They turned off Fifth Street and walked a few doors down to a hole-in-the-wall lounge named The Elbow Room, so named because it contained a bar and just enough "elbow room" to turn around. Harry stopped outside the front door.

"It was right in there," said Harry.

"What was right in there?" asked Boulder.

"Where they met."

"Where who met?" asked Boulder, growing increasingly frustrated with this little man.

"Benji and his girlfriend."

Boulder turned his head to the man. "What girlfriend?"

"The one that asked him to get married." Boulder put his hands in his pockets and burrowed his forehead in deep thought. A clinking sound in the parking lot across the street caught Harry's ear. "Look! There's an aluminum pie plate. See ya later." And off he scuttled.

Boulder stood there thinking, attempting to tie in this information. Was this a revelation? Was it relevant? What did it mean? Maybe there was someone who knew more. Boulder went inside The Elbow Room and was greeted by a blonde bartender who looked about the same age as Boulder. She had the look of someone whom a man could tell his troubles to, but who had heard it all before. There was no one else in the tiny space. Boulder could not imagine it holding more than twenty people at the same time. He introduced himself and handed her a card.

"Oh yeah," said the bartender. "We heard about you. Investigating the Newberry case, and all. Boy, that was really something, wasn't it? Digging up the body. That stuff gives me the creeps."

"I understand Benji had a girlfriend."

"Don't know about that," said the woman as she stacked the shelves behind the bar.

"Did you work here last fall?" asked Boulder. "Say September through December?"

"I did." The bartender snapped her fingers. "I know what you're getting at now. Benji used to stop by after work once or twice a week. One day this gal shows up. A real looker. Real classy, you know. So classy she doesn't belong here, if you know what I mean. I knew when she came in that she was here to meet someone. Then when Benji came in she went right next to where he was standing—right over there—and they started up a conversation.

"I figured they knew each other, but then I overheard her asking him questions about his photography. It looked to me like a spider catching a fly, if you know what I mean. They left together and I never saw either one of them again."

"When was this?"

"Let me think," she said. "It would have had to be in November." She snapped her fingers again. "I got it. It was the week of the Alabama-Mississippi State game. Benji said he was going to the game and shoot pictures of the scoreboard. He was working on a project to photograph scoreboards. Rumor has it that he and that gal went away somewhere for the weekend. And like I said, Mister, that's the last time I saw either one of them."

"Did you get her name?"

"Nope. We don't ask for names in here."

"Any idea where she came from?" asked Boulder. "Was she local?"

"Don't think so. I'd never seen her before. I would have remembered if I had," she said, and turned around and turned on a television above the bar. "How 'bout a beer? It's eleven o'clock and we're officially open."

"I believe I'll pass," said Boulder. "Thanks for your help."

Boulder had always made it a point to thank interviewees for their help, not their information. It is basic human nature to want to help someone, but against human nature to give out information about others, he reasoned. He went back outside and back up the hill to Fifth Street, then had a weird hunch. If this "spider" was after Benji, it probably meant that she was after his money. How would she be able to get his money? He walked quickly to Marcia Stockwell's office.

"I did not expect to see you back so soon," she said with a smile.

"If two people get married, they have to go somewhere and apply for a marriage license, don't they?"

"It sounds like your girlfriend has decided on the law AND you. I think she made a wise decision. Congratulations."

"No. It's not that at all," he said. "It might have something to do with the case. Where would the marriage licenses be issued?"

"That would be the circuit clerk's office. It's next door on the second floor," she said, standing up from behind her desk. "Care for some lunch first?"

"I'd love some," he said.

"What are you hungry for?"

"You know what I like?" said Boulder. "I like to go to places that the tourists haven't discovered. A place where the locals go, but don't tell everybody else."

"Sounds like Sallie's in the Alley," she said.

They walked from the courthouse complex down to Main Street, took a right and then a left on Fourth Street.

"This is Catfish Alley," she said. "So named because it smelled like catfish cooking during the lunch hour back in the twenties and thirties. It was the hub of African-American business activity at one time. The

rural black folks would come into town and sell their fruits and vegetables here. On the way, they would catch catfish and bring them along, too. Some people cooked it on a little hotplate and sold it that way. The aroma filled the air, and people who worked downtown would sneak over and buy fried catfish. All that's gone now, but there's still a good restaurant here. Here it is."

They went inside Sallie's, also known as Jones Cafe, an eatery that Boulder would have definitely described as "down-home." Brown vinyl-covered booths lined the walls, and a few tables that must have come from some-one's kitchen were strategically placed in the center of the room. Neon beer signs added a glow from above. They took seats at a booth and were instantly greeted.

"Sorry, but we're already out of the chicken-fried steak, but everything else on the menu is available. Tell me what you would like to drink, and I'll get that while you're deciding."

They both ordered iced tea. The menu was a collection of blue-plate specials. Boulder looked around and saw that the place was almost full. Their drinks were back promptly, and the server was ready for their order.

"I'll have a vegetable plate, " said Stockwell.

"The meat loaf special for me," said Boulder.

"Good choice," was the reply.

Their food arrived faster than McDonald's could serve it up. Boulder scanned the scene of blacks and whites enjoying lunch in the same restaurant. He left

Mississippi in 1968 and didn't return for twenty-five years. It was a different, better Mississippi that he came back to.

"Sounds like you have something up your sleeve," she said.

"You're not going to believe it, if what I think could have happened actually did. I'll tell you after we go to that marriage license bureau."

Forty minutes later they arrived at the circuit clerk's office, where Marcia was greeted in the manner of a familiar courthouse face by the clerk behind the counter. She explained that "this man" would like some information.

"I'd like to know if Benji Newberry filed an application for a marriage license last November," said Boulder.

"Just one moment, sir."

The clerk consulted a large, bound official book containing carbon copies of the applications. She flipped pages until she got to November. "Here's a Benjamin Whitby Newberry and Renee Lackey filed on November 20 of last year."

"May we have a copy of that?" said Marcia Stockwell.

They received the copy and looked at the address given by each applicant. Benji used his Columbus address. Renee Lackey's was given as a street and apartment number in Tuscaloosa, Alabama. They went back to Stockwell's office, and Boulder told her about his meeting Harry Ludlam and The Elbow Room bartender.

"So what do you make of this, Ms. Prosecutor?"

"I'm not sure," she said. "It could mean everything or nothing. Of course, it is very strange that she did not make her presence known at the funeral."

"That's for sure," said Boulder. "I think I need to call my lawyer on this one. May I borrow your telephone?"

"Help yourself. Would you like for me to leave?"

"No," he said. "Stay here."

"Just dial direct. This is public business."

Boulder punched in the number at Laura Webster's law firm in Jackson and asked to speak to her. When she came on the line, he briefed her on the Renee Lackey development and then asked his legal question. The answer confirmed his suspicions. He told Laura that it would be necessary for him to stay in Columbus a few more days, but would keep in touch.

"Just what I was afraid of," said Boulder to Stockwell. "If Thurston Newberry died first, then his will would be executed and Benji, OR HIS ESTATE, would receive his share. If Benji died before the father, then Benji wouldn't have any estate to get anything, assuming he was unmarried and had no heirs." He paused. "I think I'm getting that right, but I defer to you lawyers. The point is that if Benji was married, then his wife would get what was left to Benji."

"I could have told you that," said Marcia Stockwell,

then added, "We definitely need to talk to Renee Lackey."

"Before we do, allow me to have someone I know in Tuscaloosa do a quick background check on Miss Lackey or Mrs. Newberry or whomever she might be." He picked up the telephone. "One more time?"

"Of course."

He called Mitchell Investigations in Tuscaloosa. Fred Mitchell was a good investigator, and he and Boulder had known each other since serving in Vietnam. Boulder requested a public records check and any other background information that could be obtained quickly on Renee Lackey. When Mitchell asked if he could call back in a week, Boulder told him that it was really needed tomorrow morning, if possible. Boulder left Stockwell's number and told Mitchell that he would be there at two o'clock tomorrow afternoon. At the appointed time Stockwell's telephone rang, and Mitchell gave his verbal report over the speakerphone to Boulder and Stockwell.

"You sure know how to pick 'em, Jack. Renee Langston Lackey, a.k.a. Renee Langston, a.k.a. Renee Lackey Newberry, resides in Tuscaloosa, is a single mother with a four-year-old daughter. She lives in a cheap apartment, drives a six-year-old Pontiac on which she is behind two payments to the used car dealer that sold it to her. Her credit is horrible. She filed chapter seven bankruptcy five years ago. She was arrested six years ago for passing a bad check, but the case was remanded to the files. She was also arrested for prostitution three years ago in a sting operation. I can't find any record of disposition on that case. I found a news article that described her and the three other girls arrested with her as high-priced call girls. She's trying hard, though. She works two jobs—one at the university and one at night as a waitress at a gentlemen's club.

"Just for verification purposes, I followed her home last night. She got off at eleven-thirty and went straight home. An old lady opened the door for her. My guess is that the lady is her mother or aunt or some other relative because she didn't leave after Renee got home."

"Do you happen to know which department she works in at the University of Alabama?" asked Boulder.

"Let's see here." There was the sound of shuffling paper. "It looks like she is a secretary in the English department."

Chapter 17

The funeral of Norman Newberry was held at historic St. Paul's Episcopal Church on College Street. The current church building was completed in 1858, although the congregation was organized in 1837 and used a building that was completed a year later. The life of Christ, beginning with the nativity, is depicted in magnificent stained-glass windows that wrap the nave of the church. Those who admire Tiffany stained-glass windows come to St. Paul's to view one signed by Tiffany himself and dedicated in 1896. The antebellum Gothic structure also houses a wonderful Aeolean Skinner organ.

In a church half-full of mourners, the standard service was used from the Book of Common Prayer. There were no great homilies, nor did anyone detect the sniffling of noses. Norman was buried in Friendship Cemetery after a short graveside service.

Meanwhile, at the district attorney's office, Jack Boulder and Marcia Stockwell were discussing the latest revelation and what to do about it.

It did not take long for their discussion to turn into an argument.

"I want to go," insisted Marcia Stockwell.

"No," said Jack Boulder sternly.

"I need to go," said Stockwell. "If and when this case comes to trial, it is I who will be examining her on the witness stand. I need to hear her the first time she tells her story."

"Who says she is going to tell a story?"

"You know what I mean," she snapped.

"If you go, it becomes official," said Boulder. "Do you consider her a suspect in a crime committed in Lowndes County, Mississippi?"

"I won't know until I talk to her. That's the point."

"If during questioning she becomes a suspect in a

felony, does the law require you to advise her of her rights?" asked Boulder.

"Possibly."

"Don't you agree that if you are there it might complicate or jeopardize your case in court? You would probably be called as a witness."

"Are YOU going to advise her of her rights if she becomes a suspect while you alone are questioning her?"

"No," said Boulder. "I'm not a law enforcement officer with the power of arrest. I'm just a citizen."

"Oh, really?" said Stockwell. "Could it be argued that you are interviewing her at the direction of the assistant district attorney of this county? Aren't you a tool of the law in such a case?"

"Don't confuse me with facts. My mind is made up."

They had reached a stalemate and they both knew it. She took the initiative. "Let's go talk to the boss."

They went upstairs and each made his or her case to the district attorney, who was already familiar with the case, having been briefed daily by Stockwell. At the suggestion—Boulder would have termed it insistence—of the district attorney it was agreed that Boulder would go to Tuscaloosa the next day and interview Renee Lackey Newberry in the company of an investigator from the district attorney's office in Tuscaloosa. She would be advised at the outset that a criminal investigation was being conducted and advised of her rights. If she chose to demand an attorney, they would ask the name of her attorney and then leave. The D.A. in Mississippi would follow up and arrange for formal questioning thereafter. If she decided to talk they would listen to her story and then call Marcia Stockwell, who would confer with her boss. They discussed other permutations and combinations of interview techniques and outcomes. Soon arrangements were made.

At nine o'clock Jack Boulder and Investigator Robert Tappan of the local district attorney's office pulled into the parking lot of Renee Lackey Newberry's apartment complex. It was a Saturday morning, so she should not be at work at either job. They got out of the unmarked government car and walked to her front door. Boulder knocked three times. Tappan's head rotated left, then right as if he was on some major drug raid. A very attractive blonde with shoulder-length hair opened the door. She wore tight blue jeans and an Alabama sweatshirt. She was barefooted and stood on one foot while balancing the other against a knee. She might have been thirty.

"Renee?" said Boulder.

"Yes."

Tappan produced a badge case and displayed his credentials. Boulder just stood there.

"We would like to talk to you about Benji Newberry," said Boulder.

She wilted. Boulder was afraid she was about to faint. She turned a head and looked over her shoulder.

Her bottom lip quivered.

"I knew this day would come," she said dejectedly. "Can we go somewhere else for this? My mother and child are here and there's not much room." Tappan looked and Boulder, who nodded. "Let me get a jacket and some shoes."

Boulder was not about to let her out of his sight. This was how people committed suicide when they knew they had no more hope. "I'll need to stay with you when you get your jacket."

"That's okay. Come on in," she said. To an older woman sitting in a recliner she said, "Mom, I'm going down to the office for a while. I'll be back before long."

The mother did not say anything. Renee opened a closet door and pulled out a light jacket. She slipped on a pair of sneakers and walked out and got in the backseat of the car as if she had foreseen this day. They drove to the district attorney's office. She was advised of her rights by Tappan and then signed a pre-printed document waiving them. A hand-held tape recorder was placed on the table. Boulder asked an open-ended question to begin the interview.

"Would you please tell us about you and Benji Newberry?"

"Can I say something first?"

"Of course," said Boulder.

"I have a four-year-old daughter and an ex-husband who has to be taken to court every month for child support. I do the best I can, but it's very tough for me. Okay?"

"I understand, " said Boulder.

"Last October I was made an offer that I couldn't refuse. I would be given ten thousand dollars if I could get Benji Newberry to marry me. Then he would be involved in an accident, and I would receive the proceeds of an insurance policy or will or something, then I would get a hundred thousand dollars and the other person would get the rest of it."

"You knew he was going to be murdered!" said Tappan, and received a scolding look from Boulder.

"I'm sorry," said Boulder. "Go ahead." Another glance at Tappan.

"Yes, I knew that it was planned that he be murdered, but I had another plan. I would take the ten thousand, then tell him it was a big mistake and that somebody was trying to kill him. The marriage would be annulled, I would take ten thousand and go to Tennessee, and Benji would deal with his own problems. Look, man, I was desperate. I needed money for my kid. But I would never let anybody get killed. I just thought I could outsmart them."

"Them who?" asked Boulder.

"Erica and whoever she was working with."

"Erica?"

"Dr. Erica Castle. One of my bosses at the university."

"So how did you get Benji to marry you?" asked Boulder.

"It was easy," she said. "He's a man, ain't he? I just showed a little interest in him and went with the flow."

"How did you meet him?"

"Erica told me about a little joint he went to most every day, so I just hung out until he showed up. It didn't take but two days."

"I understand you had a nice weekend," said Boulder.

"We sure did," she said. "He got to talking about how he liked beaches, so we took off for Gulf Shores and spent the weekend there. By Sunday morning he had proposed. I didn't even have to bring it up. We went back to Columbus and did what we needed to do to get the marriage license."

"Where were you married?"

"Livingston, Alabama, of course. There's a judge down there that's married half of Mississippi and Alabama."

"When was this?" asked Boulder.

"I believe it was the Tuesday before Thanksgiving."

"Geez," sighed Tappan. "She doesn't even remember her wedding date." Another scowl from Boulder.

"Where did you spend Wednesday and Thursday?" asked Boulder.

"I came back to Tuscaloosa and told Erica that the mission had been accomplished. She made me show her the papers."

"When did she give you the money?"

"Right then," she said. "That would have been the

day before Thanksgiving. Benji called me that night and told me he wanted me to come back to Columbus so that he could introduce me to his family on Thanksgiving Day. I went there on Wednesday and stayed with him that night. He got up early to go hunting and never came back."

"How did you find out about his death?"

"It was all over the news on WCBI-TV at noon. I panicked and got back in my car and came back home. I didn't know what to do."

"Did you go to work on Monday?" asked Boulder.

"Yes. I saw Erica and she said that I did a good job and that as soon as things were settled I would be a hundred thousand dollars richer. I made a bad mistake, but I didn't have anything to do with his killing. You've got to believe me."

They continued the interview for another hour, filling in details, confirming her statements about their whereabouts. Investigator Tappan was flabbergasted. He had never seen anything like this. Boulder took it in stride. Just another sad case of people's disregard for other human beings.

Afterwards, Boulder telephoned Marcia Stockwell and gave her the details of the interview. Tappan agreed to hold Renee Lackey Newberry pending extradition to Mississippi. Boulder took the tape and drove back to Columbus, arriving in mid-afternoon. He played it for the district attorney and for Marcia Stockwell.

"Looks like you are going to get your first big case," said the district attorney. "Marcia, make preparations to have Dr. Erica Newberry Castle indicted for conspiracy to commit murder."

Chapter 18

It was a busy Sunday in the district attorney's office. Marcia Stockwell worked all day on her first big case—rather cases. It was decided that since the grand jury was already in session, the case of Nathanial Newberry and the case of Erica Newberry Castle would be presented on Monday. Stockwell presented more than enough evidence. On Tuesday morning Nathanial Newberry was indicted for the murder of Norman Newberry, and Erica Newberry Castle was indicted for conspiracy to commit murder of Benjamin Whitby Newberry. Warrants were issued and by six o'clock that evening the Newberry brother and sister were in jail awaiting arrangements for bail.

Gardner Johnson, attorney at law, had been the Newberry family lawyer for over forty years. He was a civil lawyer who preferred working on matters such as partnership agreements and estate planning. He almost always referred criminal matters of any kind to other lawyers in town. He believed that lawyers best served the community when they helped parties reach agreement and solve their problems instead of suing each other. He was a robust man going on seventy years, with red hair and a friendly manner. One of the little known facts in Columbus was that he played Santa Claus each year in the Christmas parade. He and Thurston Newberry, his best client, always met after the parade and had warm drinks in the Newberry mansion until late in the evening.

He had received the call from Ethel Newberry while watching the evening news coverage of the Market Street Festival. A nationally known teenage boys group was the featured attraction this year and crowd control was a topic of concern. Ethel commanded him to go to the jail and bail out her two remaining children. Johnson detected a slur in her voice and wondered if she had gotten into the gin again. He wanted to tell her that he was too old to handle cases like this one. She insisted and he desisted with his objections. His own two children had been put though college just on the legal fees he collected from the Newberry children's legal matters. He knew the call would come sooner or later after he had heard last week that Norman had killed Benji.

"Evening, Mr. Johnson," said the jailer. "Bet I know who you have come for."

"How much is their bond, Olson? Or is it still possible for people to be released on personal recognizance?"

The jailer checked some records and said, "You need to see Judge Featherstone."

Johnson walked down the hall to the office of Justice Court Judge Presley Featherstone and asked, "How much, Pres?"

"A hundred thousand for Nate and two hundred fifty thousand for her. She lives out of state."

The attorney detected a smugness in the magistrate's voice. "How much you think the Newberry mansion is worth?"

"Twice that much."

"I understand you have some property bond forms."

The judge reached in a desk drawer and laid a legal-sized printed document on his desk.

"Where do I sign?" asked Johnson.

"Take it to Mrs. Newberry and have her sign it. Then bring it back to me. I'll authorize their release then."

"I have power-of-attorney," he replied, pulling a pen from his pocket. "Just show me where to sign."

The justice court judge pointed to the blanks that needed filling out and waited patiently with his arms folded. Once their business was done and the rest of the paperwork completed, Nate and Erica were released to Johnson. He instructed them to go to the Newberry mansion, saying he would be along shortly. They could take a taxi if necessary.

Gardner Johnson cursed under his breath, not so much for his disdain of their alleged deeds but for the fact that they had called him in the first place. He was getting too old for this. He headed back down the hall and noticed a young woman standing in a doorway. She stuck out a hand.

"Mr. Johnson, I'm Marcia Stockwell, assistant district attorney."

"Thank goodness. Is there some place we can talk?"

"Follow me to my office."

Once inside her office she briefed him on what had happened, then gave him copies of the indictments. She then invited Boulder to come inside and join their conversation.

"First, I want you to know that I am their family lawyer. I'll be engaging a criminal attorney to assist me," he said with as much authority as he could muster.

They chatted for a few more minutes, then Johnson said that he needed to leave to go to the Newberry mansion, "to tend to my flock."

"Mr. Johnson," said Boulder, as they stood up. "Do you have a copy of Thurston Newberry's will?"

"A copy? No. I have the original."

The three of them stood there for a moment, waiting for someone to be first to say something. Johnson obliged.

"I really must go now. My clients need me."

"Wait a minute," said Marcia Stockwell, placing a hand on his arm. "When was the will filed for probate?" She turned to Boulder and said, "We may have a copy right here at the courthouse."

"I'm afraid not," said Johnson. "Ethel Newberry told

me at the funeral not to do anything with the will until she instructed me. I always follow my client's instructions."

"What does the will say?" asked Boulder.

"Please. I need to attend to my clients," said Johnson. "The will is fairly long and involved."

"With all due respect, Mr. Johnson, the will goes to the heart of the motive in this case. It will be subpoenaed anyway, plus it will become public record very soon even if it is not subpoenaed. We really want to see that will immediately."

"How about first thing in my office tomorrow morning? I'll probably be tied up a long time tonight."

"Very well," said Stockwell. "We will be at your office at eight o'clock tomorrow morning."

Gardner Johnson departed. Boulder and Stockwell returned to their discussion.

"What are you thinking, Jack?"

"We have been presuming that this was all about the changing of the will, and the three children getting cut out." He strummed his fingers on the table. "What if we have presumed in error?"

"Explain."

"Well, what if Thurston Newberry wasn't really rich after all? What if he was deep in debt and really had no money?"

"Unlikely."

"What if the will doesn't leave any of the children

anything?"

"Jack, I think we know what the will says."

"Perhaps," he replied, and stood up. "I'll meet you here at seven-thirty tomorrow morning."

Boulder left and Marcia Stockwell returned to the lawbooks. Her yellow legal pad was filling up with notes about how to prosecute the cases. An ever-so-small amount of exhilaration rose up in her. She loved this work.

The next morning, Boulder and Stockwell arrived at Johnson's richly furnished Lawyers' Row office and were ushered to the conference room by the reception-ist. Momentarily, the door opened and Gardner Johnson entered the room, accompanied by Ethel Newberry. They sat down and Boulder studied the matron of the family. She looked like she had spent the night outside the intensive care unit of a hospital. Her eyes were swollen and red, and Boulder detected sags in her face that he had not noticed before. She wore a black dress and stared straight ahead, eyes staring through the wall. Her chin was up, like a soldier in basic training.

Johnson handed Boulder and Stockwell a multi-page document on legal-sized paper.

"What you have in front of you is Thurston Newberry's last will and testament," he said. "As you can see, it is dated March fifteenth of last year." He paused and allowed the information to sink in. "If you will turn to page eighteen, which has already been tabbed for you, it will be noted what Thurston Newberry provided for his children."

They studied the single line that was highlighted in yellow. The key phrase jumped out: ". . . my remaining assets to be divided equally among my four children, Norman, Nathanial, Erica, and Benjamin."

As if on cue, Boulder and Stockwell snapped their heads up and looked at Ethel Newberry. She remained locked in position.

"You are certain that this is the final will?" asked Stockwell.

"I have drafted every will Thurston Newberry ever had. And there were many. If he had another will or if there was a codicil, it would have been forwarded to me by now."

"So Mrs. Newberry wasn't telling me the truth when she said that the will had been changed last August," Boulder pointed out.

"That would be correct," replied Johnson.

"And she was not telling the truth to her children when she told them that her husband had modified the will," said Boulder.

"I have asked her to come here and explain that." He turned to her and said, "Ethel."

She lowered her jaw and looked back and forth to Boulder and Stockwell.

"I made a terrible mistake," she said, her voice cracking. "Gardner, could I have a glass of water?"

Johnson got up, opened the door slightly, and whispered to an assistant. They waited a long minute until the glass of water was delivered and Ethel Newberry continued.

"I thought that by telling Norman and Nate and Erica that their father had reduced their inheritance then they would show him the attention he needed and deserved. I told every one of them to come see their father. You can check my telephone records. I called Erica every week last summer and early fall, trying to get her to drive over and see her father. It's not very far from Tuscaloosa to Columbus, you know." She took a sip of water. "You people do not have any idea of what it is like to live with someone who thinks that he is going to die any day. Such people fret and become depressed. They feel abandoned and they imagine things. Every day I prayed that those children would come by or call. Benji was the only one who gave Thurston any attention.

"All of this is my fault. I hope you understand that my children would not have done what they did had it not been for me. That's all I want you to know. This is all my fault."

With that statement, she burst into tears and began shaking. Johnson got up and summoned an assistant, directing her to take Ethel Newberry to his office and stay with her. After she left the room, Johnson sat back down.

"I thought you needed to hear that," he said. "I

believe it explains quite a bit." Johnson paused before continuing. "Ms. Stockwell, I appreciate the job you have to do. I want you to know that after discussions last night I am also representing Erica and Nathanial. I also want you to know that Nathanial is willing to plead guilty to manslaughter. He is willing to serve a minimum sentence, but frankly I do not think he is up to it. He has been taken to Jackson and admitted to a recovery center. If I may be so bold to say, I don't think you could even get a conviction for murder. Your best evidence is a statement from Norman's wife, I understand."

"I will discuss your offer with the district attorney," said Stockwell. "What about Erica?"

"She is willing to plead guilty to a misdemeanor, but not a felony."

"Unacceptable."

"I thought that would be your reaction. I will advise her to retain a criminal lawyer for her defense."

Chapter 19

Jack Boulder and Marcia Stockwell walked back over to the courthouse annex and reported the morning's developments to the district attorney. He immediately agreed to accept a plea bargain for Nathanial. He then directed Stockwell to "prosecute Erica Newberry Castle to the fullest extent of the law." The two returned to Stockwell's office.

"Tell me how you lay out this case," she said to Boulder.

"It's a murder case so let's begin with motive, means, and opportunity. The motive, of course, is the belief that she was cut out of the will and was not going to receive millions of dollars of inheritance. The original conspiracy was with Norman, who agreed to kill Benji on the deer hunt. It might be stretching it to believe that he could set it up that way, but when you show all the circumstances, such as the placement of Robbie, the gun that he used, and the statements he made blaming Robbie . . ."

"What about the possibility that they would not even see a deer?" she interjected.

"Good question. I'll bet you can find witnesses who can testify that Norman was a deer hunting expert. He knew that deer are creatures of habit and walk along a certain cut-through every morning at a certain time. You might be able to find someone who could put Norman at that location scouting out deer movements the week before. But the pistol and the photographs are the best proof of Norman's intentions. When the jury looks at that print of Norman aiming at Benji's camera, they will get the picture—pun intended," he said with a grin.

She was taking notes on her legal pad as he talked.

"Back up just a minute," she said. "That might very

well prove Norman to be a killer. When did he and Erica plot this conspiracy?"

"You might need some additional research on that point. Telephone records, whatever. Renee will be the key witness who ties in Norman and Erica. Don't forget to protect her at all costs. In my opinion, she would do or say anything for money."

"There is another issue here," said Stockwell. "Since Renee was apparently Benji's wife, she might be entitled to his estate, assuming that he did not have a will. Of course, the civil side of this case will be all about the time of death. If the Newberrys can prove that Benji died first, she would get nothing. But if the father died first . . ."

"That is unbelievable," said Boulder "Wait 'til she finds out she might be a multimillionaire."

"I'm hoping that Gardner Johnson will sort out the civil side of all this," she said.

"The litigation will go on for years when the shark lawyers hear about this case."

"It is all so very ironic," she mused.

"How so?"

"From four children and a wealthy father to two dead children, one mentally-weakened brother, and a sister awaiting a felony trial. All because they would not show a little concern for their father."

"Are you asking: Where did it all go wrong?"

"You might say that," she replied.

"A manipulative mother," said Boulder. "I think she enjoyed it just a little too much, and things got out of hand."

They talked on for another hour, discovering that each part of this case produced a new revelation and a new irony. Marcia Stockwell had her work cut out for her.

"I'm heading back to Jackson," said Boulder, standing up. "I'll be available if you need me."

"I just thought of something," she said, laying her pen down on the pad. "Erica Newberry was your client. Who is going to pay you?"

"I'll send her a bill. We will see what happens. She said she wanted to know if her brother's death was an accident. I believe I found the answer to that."

"One last question," said Stockwell, her mouth widening to a soft smile. "Are you going to ask her to marry you?"

"Yes," he said. "This case has made me realize how important true relationships can be. I'm getting nervous just thinking about it."

"You will do fine. Good luck, Jack Boulder."

He drove away from Columbus into one of the most radiant sunsets he had ever seen.

Chapter 20

The next evening Laura Webster and Jack Boulder supped on a fabulous meal at the University Club, high atop the Capital City's tallest building. He wore his only suit, a navy blue model, and a colorful red necktie that Laura had gotten him for Christmas last year. After the main course, the server wheeled a dessert cart to their table and tempted them with many choices. He succumbed to the cheesecake, she to the Mississippi Mud Pie. All that was left to do was for him to say the words. He had thought about getting an engagement ring, but decided it would be more fun for the two of them to pick out one.

"Laura, there is something I want to say. Something this Columbus case made me realize."

"Oh, Jack," she smiled. She was aglow in beauty tonight. "There is something I realized while you were away. Can I tell you first?"

"By all means," he said. Thank goodness.

"When you were gone it was like you were here. Like you were a part of me. I thought about our relationship and what we have. I confess that when you moved back to Mississippi and we started dating, I secretly hoped that it would lead to marriage. You would be the perfect husband for me.

"But now I have come to realize that marriage would

probably spoil it. What we have right now is more blissful than marriage. When you said you never wanted to get married again I took offense. Now I find that you were wise. We are perfect for each other as we are. And I just want to say that I love you, Jack Boulder."

He took a sip of water for his tight throat and said, "I could not have said it better." He slowly placed the glass back on the table. "I've got an idea. Let's go to the Pilgrimage in Columbus."

"Great idea."

EPILOGUE

The murder conspiracy trial of Erica Newberry Castle took five days. She was convicted and is now serving time in the state penitentiary.

Afterwards the *Commercial Dispatch* carried the following editorial:

The Newberry murder and conspiracy cases that have rocked Columbus for the past months are finally over, and there is no more doubt in the minds of our citizens as to what occurred. This is due in large part to the excellent trial preparation and work of Assistant District Attorney Marcia Stockwell. She went up against a pair of the best criminal defense lawyers in two states and showed that being a rookie prosecutor is no hindrance. She is a native of the Gulf Coast, but let's hope that she makes her career in Columbus.

Nathanial Newberry spent three months at the recovery center. He pled guilty to manslaughter and was sentenced to five years in prison, with four years and seven months suspended pending his good behavior. He was given credit for the time spent in the recovery center. He returned to management of the furniture store, and he and his family are progressing well at getting their lives back together. They gave ten percent of Nathanial's inheritance to the church and invested the rest.

Renee Lackey Newberry was terminated from her secretarial position. She testified in the trial and then moved to Tennessee with her mother and daughter. She now sells beauty supplies. She has retained legal counsel and filed suit for her share of the Newberry fortune.

Earlene Newberry sold the cabin and all of the land owned by her husband, Norman, and moved into a large, second-story apartment on Main Street. She is a plaintiff and a defendant in the continuing litigation.

Ethel Newberry is driven by Tessie to Friendship Cemetery on Sundays and Fridays. A lawn chair is removed from the trunk of the car. She sits down and meditates for twenty minutes near the graves of her husband and two sons. She never misses a service at St. Paul's.

As expected, the civil cases go on.